COZY MYSTERIES FOR FALL

DAISY LANDISH

Editing by Rachael Lammie
Cover by Daisy Landish

First Edition

BEACHES AND TRAILS
PUBLISHING

ABOUT THE AUTHOR

Daisy Landish is a romance and cozy mystery author living in the UK, whose clean and sweet stories have tugged at readers' heartstrings across the pond and beyond. When she's not writing, Daisy spends her time reading, hiking at dawn, and riding into the sunset on her horse, Rosebud.

Join Daisy's Newsletter for updates and giveaways!
www.daisylandishromance.com

facebook.com/daisylandishromance

x.com/daisy_landish

instagram.com/beachesandtrailspublishing

amazon.com/author/daisylandish

bookbub.com/authors/daisy-landish

goodreads.com/Daisy_Landish

ALSO BY DAISY LANDISH

Clean Regency Romance

The Lady Series - The Allington Collection

The Lady Series - The Gillingham Collection

The Lady Series - The Blackmore Collection

The Lady Series - The Norrington Collection

Clean Contemporary Romance

Love on Spruce Island

Second Chance

Cherry Tree Island

The Wedding Trio

Extra Credit

Counting on the Cowboy

Focusing on the Cowboy

Mistletoe Magic

Grounded at Christmas

Cozy Mysteries

Jane and Kennedy Daniels Mysteries

Pine Grove Mysteries

Annie Archer Paranormal Mysteries

Wilma Wade Holiday Mysteries

Mike and Maddie Mysteries

Mystic Moonhaven Mysteries

Sweater Weather: Cozy Mysteries for Fall

Summer Vibes: Cozy Mysteries for Summer

Let it Snow: Cozy Mysteries for Winter

TAKING THE FALL

A MIKE AND MADDIE MYSTERY

PROLOGUE

Mike sat at his typewriter. It was old-fashioned, and he liked how it felt to type on it. Oh, he was quicker with a computer. But with the spring storm thundering outside and a chill in the air as winter slowly faded away, he had turned off the power in his home and lit a few candles for the ambiance he sought.

He had had a dream about a spooky paranormal mystery that he wanted desperately to write about. Unfortunately, it was one of those rare times that his well of imagination was dry.

He leaned back in this chair, his fingers resting on the worn keys of his typewriter. What was preventing him from writing?

Maybe it was that his closest friend, Maddie Moreau, was currently out to dinner with the handsome, well-known author Ben Hiddlestone.

No, that couldn't be it. While Mike would have liked to have been there, he wasn't jealous and was glad that Maddie had found another friend she could spend time with. He got along well with Ben, too. He didn't come to Coeur D'Alene very often, and it had been Mike who turned down his dinner invitation.

He needed to get this book written.

"So what is stopping me?" he wondered aloud.

Mike had often found he was better at figuring out problems if he spoke aloud, even if he only talked to himself.

His neighbors thought he was a strange fellow. Mike honestly thought it was quite funny and enjoyed making them believe he was even weirder than he was.

"If I'm not feeling left out of Maddie and Ben's dinner, maybe I'm hungry?" He mentally probed how he was feeling. "No, that's not it. I should get some water, though."

Pushing himself from his table, he went to the kitchen and got himself water. As he drank it, he thought more about his predicament.

Sighing, he shook his head. "No, I know exactly what is preventing me from writing. It's the Harding case."

A young woman, Katelyn Harding, had recently gone missing. Her family was convinced that it was her husband, but there was no evidence that the police could find that Katelyn was even dead. Mike was sure she was and that the husband had killed her.

The whole town was aflutter with the rumors of it, but no evidence to put the husband behind bars had been uncovered. Mike knew it wasn't his responsibility… but he just wished he could figure this out.

Only once the killer was arrested could he write this novel.

CHAPTER 1

The bite of frost in the air was delicious. Mike breathed in the scent as he walked along the path near the long lake Coeur D'Alene was built next to. Fall was a delightful time of year, with the trees having changed color and dead leaves crunching underfoot. Best of all, Halloween was approaching.

Oh, it was still too early for the decorations to have been brought out. But black cats, ghosts, and skeletons would soon be abounding.

Mike loved Halloween.

He came to a bench that looked over the lake and eased himself into it. He had been walking for over an hour, simply enjoying the weather. The sun beamed overhead, bringing with it the promise of another hot day. Cold in the mornings, pleasant at noon, fading to cold again at night. It was almost like all four seasons wrapped up in one day.

His phone dinged, announcing a text message. He pulled the device from his pocket, checking it. He'd received a message from his friend Detective Carson Luttrell.

Dinner at my place tonight. Burgers and beer. You in?

Sure thing!

Mike had to smile. Usually, his tastes ran a little more sophisticated than burgers and beer, but occasionally, he indulged in his childhood's wonderful tastes. When he was a kid growing up on a farm in the middle of nowhere, they had little.

He was confident that his current tastes were more because he didn't have the resources to drink expensive wines and eat filet mignon back then. He loved the freedom to buy such costly things. It reminded him that he no longer had one foot in poverty.

The barking of a dog drew his attention, and he looked up. It was a golden retriever, tail wagging as it ran toward him.

"Copper!" a woman running behind the retriever yelled. "Copper!"

The retriever, Copper, skidded to a stop. Its tail continued to wag, but it looked between Mike and the woman as though confused about what to do. Mike couldn't help but chuckle.

"Copper, come here," the woman yelled.

The retriever turned and trotted back to the woman. She grabbed his leash and shook her head, murmuring to the dog before she looked up at Mike.

"I'm sorry," she called. "I promise he's friendly. He was looking to make a new friend."

Mike stood. "It's all right. I had a lot of retrievers when I was a kid. I know what they're like. Can I say hello?"

The woman smiled as she approached. "Sure thing. Copper here would love that."

Mike walked over and crouched, scratching behind the dog's ears. Copper leaned into his scratch, his tongue lolling out and tail wagging even faster.

"You're a good boy, aren't you?" Mike crooned.

"He is when he listens," the woman agreed. "I only got him a few weeks ago from a rescue, but he's trying his best to learn. My name is Beatrice. Beatrice Eden. But I prefer to be called Tricia. I know it's not exactly a common nickname with Beatrice, but—"

She suddenly went silent, blushing.

Mike laughed as he straightened. "I don't know that it makes much difference. You like to be called Tricia; I'll call you Tricia. I'm Michael Malison, but you can call me Mike."

"Please to meet you, Mike." Tricia held out her hand, and Mike shook it. "I haven't seen you around the park before. Are you new?"

"No. I've lived here for quite a few years, but I usually walk on the other side of the lake. Do you mind if I walk with you for a bit? I miss having a dog. Can't keep one myself, allergies." Mike's face twisted. Itchy eyes and a stuffed-up head were nothing to laugh about.

Tricia's eyes widened. "Oh! I'm sorry if I'd known—"

"No, no, nothing to apologize for," Mike said. "They're too bad to deal with daily but not bad enough to give up a chance to pet one when the opportunity presents itself. Believe me, I'm willing to deal with the symptoms in the open air."

"I was going to let him go for a swim. The day's getting warmer, and there won't be many of them left," Tricia said.

Mike looked around and picked up a stick. "Mind if I play some fetch?"

Copper pranced on the spot; his eyes locked on the stick.

Tricia laughed as she unhooked his leash. "Go ahead."

With a mighty throw, the stick spun through the air, landing on the grassy field some distance away. Copper waited until it landed before he bolted forward, rushing to the fallen stick. He picked it up and trotted back to Mike and Tricia. He gently laid it down at Tricia's feet.

She picked up the stick and threw it.

"There are hypoallergenic dogs, you know," she said, laughing as she watched her dog. "If you really wanted one."

"I know," Mike said. "I've spent time with them… allergic to them, too. It's a curse."

"Ugh, I'm so sorry," Tricia said sympathetically.

Copper stopped near a copse of bushes.

"Bring the stick back," Tricia called.

Copper sniffed at the bushes, then backed away, whining. He barked quietly at first but grew in frequency and pitch.

Tricia and Mike glanced at each other in alarm. Copper kept barking, and they both rushed forward. Tricia grabbed Copper's collar and hauled him back, quickly clipping the leash back. The dog pressed into her legs, whining, and shaking now.

"What is it?" Tricia asked with her eyes on the bush.

Mike bent, peering into the dense foliage. The bushes were right against the water's edge, the lake lapping at their roots. Something bright yellow caught his eye. Mike crept closer, tense and ready to jump aside if something like a fox or raccoon attacked him out of self-defense.

His heart dropped to his stomach when a hand appeared beneath the bushes. It was pale, white. Yellow nail polish glimmered in the morning light.

Mike had seen enough bodies to know that this one was dead from just the color. He straightened and turned back to Tricia. "Call 9-1-1 and tell them we've found a body."

"What?" Tricia gasped. "A body?"

"Yes. Please hurry." Mike pulled his phone from his pocket. Then, to make sure Tricia knew he wasn't also calling 9-1-1, he added, "I have a friend in the police department. I'll phone him so he can get out here ASAP."

Tricia, visibly shaking now, dialed the emergency number while Mike called Carson. The detective answered after a few rings.

"Yes, it has to be burgers and beers," Carson laughed.

It took Mike a moment to understand what he was talking about. Right, the dinner. He shook his head, sighing. "No, it's not about that. I'm at the beach, and I've found a body."

He walked around the bushes, bracing himself to see what he would find on the other side. His heart dropped as he saw a young woman dressed in a bright yellow dress, the sort you'd see on women in the 1950s.

"A body?" Carson's tone immediately turned serious and business-like. "Where?"

Mike told him his location, then described what he could see. A young woman with chocolate-brown hair was lying face down among the bushes, partly in the water. It lapped at her skirt, making the fabric flare like she was still breathing.

"Are you sure she's dead?" Carson asked.

By the sounds, Mike knew he was rushing around, getting ready to head out. "She's dead, Carson. No living person has that color. There's another person here calling 9-1-1."

"Good," Carson said. "I'll be there in ten minutes."

"Thanks." Mike hung up, breathing deeply.

His day had certainly just taken a turn.

Tricia was still on the phone, and Mike hesitated as he flipped to Maddie's number. She had been in the zone when he left her apartment, so intent on her writing that she had hardly noticed when he'd made her a fresh cup of coffee.

Did he really want to interrupt her for this?

Mike sighed as he sent a text instead, telling her to call him if she had a moment. If it were him, he would want Maddie and Carson to let him know, but he would also want to be left alone. This was better; it allowed Maddie to interrupt herself or choose to reply.

Carson was at the lake in ten minutes, and soon after, more police and various emergency responders were there. Carson took control of the scene, and Mike helped set up a barrier, then retreated to stand near Tricia, kneeling next to Copper with her face buried in his golden-red fur.

"Are you all right?" he asked her.

"Oh, I'm all right," Tricia sighed. "I just never thought I'd find a body. It must be that young woman who went missing last week. What was her name? Carla Fletcher? I knew she'd be found dead. I just... I hope it's not her."

Mike patted Tricia's shoulder, trying to be comforting. Everyone knew about Carla Fletcher's disappearance. Her husband had been on the news, begging her to come home. He kept claiming that she had run off.

The darker whispers had said something far worse had happened to her.

Carson headed over to them, his expression grave.

"Is it..." Mike asked, his tone worried.

Carson nodded once. "Carla Fletcher. The ME thinks she died around midnight. But there's more, Mike... can we talk privately?"

CHAPTER 2

"What is it, Carson?" Mike asked, glancing toward the bushes where the body was.

"First, are you all right?" Concern filled Carson's expression.

Mike took a moment to assess himself. He was shaken, for sure, but he had already compartmentalized these events. His concern had been more for Tricia than himself. He rubbed his itchy eyes and realized why Carson was so concerned. His eyes were streaming, red, and puffy.

"Allergies," Mike explained. "I'm allergic to the dog, but I've been ignoring that to ensure Tricia is all right."

Carson's shoulders slumped slightly. "You're all right, then?"

"Yes, I believe so. It's not exactly run of the mill, but I'm ready to answer your questions." Mike straightened himself, resisting the urge to rub his eyes again. He rolled back his shoulders, feeling the tension lingering in his body. "So, what do you need me to do?"

Carson eyed him for a moment longer before he nodded once as though satisfied with Mike's answer. "We found Kevin Fletcher's body this morning. He was bashed in the head by something long and thin, like a crowbar. The ME's initial examination of Carla Fletcher's body shows a similar end to her."

That couldn't be a coincidence. Husband and wife both killed in the same fashion? Did that indicate the husband wasn't guilty, as everyone —including Mike—had assumed?

On the other hand,… "When was Carla killed? Is it possible that they somehow killed each other?"

"No, no. Kevin's body was still warm when found; we received an early morning call about his murder in his home. It's impossible that Carla could have smashed him over the head with him still being able to dump her body before returning to his home."

"How long?" Mike took a deep breath, bracing himself. He hadn't seen enough of Carla's body to guess how long she'd been dead.

Carson shook his head. "At least a day."

"Isn't it possible, then, for Kevin to have received the blow to his head, kill Carla, dump her body, then return to his home and die from the previous blow?" Mike suggested.

"No."

Mike opened his mouth to ask how Carson could be so sure but shut it again. There was only one reason for that certainty without a complete autopsy. The damage to Kevin Fletcher's head had to be too great to allow him to have survived anything.

"All right," Mike finally said. "So, Carla Fletcher was killed at least a day ago, and Kevin Fletcher was killed this morning. This might be the work of a serial killer, then. Someone who targets young couples?"

Carson's expression grew even grimmer. "I believe we are. I haven't told you, but there is something even more unsettling."

"What is it?"

"Later," Carson murmured as Tricia approached, clutching her dog's leash. "I will tell you and Maddie at the same time."

Waiting wasn't exactly a strong suit of Mike's, but he understood the need to wait. Although thinking of Maddie now made him realize he hadn't contacted his writing partner. As Tricia talked to Carson, Mike took a few steps away.

We'll need to reschedule the plan for today, he wrote. *The body of Carla Fletcher has been found. Carson and I will be around later to discuss it.*

He thought about writing that he had been the one to find the body, but that would be better to discuss in person. The details about the yellow 50's dress, both Carla and Kevin being murdered in the same way, and this mysterious 'unsettling' information that Carson was loath to share was adding up to bring a shiver in Mike's spine.

A moment later, Maddie replied. *Let me know when you're on your way. I'll have coffee and food for you both.*

Mike smiled softly to himself. Coffee and food were the perfect thing to discuss the case over.

"I don't have any other questions for you at the moment," Carson told Tricia. "If you think of anything else I should know, you can call me at this number."

He handed over a business card, then glanced over at Mike. "And if it's something that you aren't certain is relevant, you can bring it up to Mike. He often works with me on my cases and will have a better idea of whether to share it with me."

A look almost like a smile played about Carson's lips. Tricia, for her part, flushed and looked pleased. She took her leave, and Mike walked with her to the end of the path.

"If you need to talk about what happened, let me know," Mike told her. He patted Copper's head. "And keep up the good work with this good boy."

"I will, on both counts," Tricia replied.

"Thank you."

Carson nodded to Mike to follow him, and the two went to Carson's car. Once they were heading for Maddie's apartment, Mike took the time to study his friend. The detective was a master at controlling his emotions and never losing his cool. Today he looked stressed, however.

It couldn't be good. The captain of Carson's precinct didn't like how Carson often had Mike and Maddie help him with his cases. Was that the cause of his stress today, or was it the case itself?

They arrived at Maddie's apartment. As soon as they stepped inside, the scent of fresh coffee and quiche met Mike's nostrils. His mouth watered; he had eaten nothing yet, and the smell of food reminded him of how hungry he was. He quickly went to the kitchen and pulled plates from the cupboard.

"I already set the table," Maddie said, shooing him off.

"Oh… you didn't have to go through the trouble," Mike started.

Maddie waved a hand. "The quiche was already in the oven, and it's not like making coffee and setting the table takes any time. Go sit down, and I'll finish up here."

Mike smiled at her. Her chocolate-brown hair was pulled back into a braid this morning. Her oversized sweatshirt slipped off one shoulder to reveal a second sweatshirt beneath it. It wasn't even that cold of a day today.

"Is that a fashion choice, or should I make you go to the doctor?" Mike asked, stepping aside for Maddie to work.

She frowned at him, silently questioning him.

"You're always so cold, and you're wearing two sweaters. Should I be worried about your health? There could be several reasons you'd be cold when it's not that cold."

Maddie gave him the indulgent, amused smile that always made his heart skip half a beat. "I'm not cold. I just wanted to coziness. Actually, I got too hot earlier and opened up the windows to make it colder in here."

Mike shook his head but smiled.

At Maddie's urging, he sat at the table. Maddie served up the quiche, coffee, and toast. Mike started eating eagerly, enjoying the savory taste on his tongue. He thought he was eating fast, but he was only half done when he looked up to find that Carson was serving himself a second piece.

"Have you been neglecting to feed yourself again?" Maddie asked severely.

"Only because I know you're such a superb cook," the detective replied with a smirk.

Maddie leaned her elbows on the table as she bit off a sizeable chunk of her toast. "Hmm. I'll be flattered enough to let you get away with that. Now, what's about this case?"

Carson ate again with gusto. Mike laid down his fork. He explained about finding Carla Fletcher's body and the added death of Kevin

Fletcher the same morning. As she listened, Maddie's expression became grimmer and grimmer.

Once Mike was done, he picked up his coffee and took a big gulp. Somehow recounting the events made him even more exhausted than he had been moments ago.

"And before we came here, Carson said he had even more unsettling information to give us," he finished, then sipped his coffee again. His dark eyes moved to the detective's face and remained unwavering on him.

Carson, by this time, had finished his second piece of quiche. He eyed the remainders with apparent hunger. But when he looked up between the two writers, his shoulders sagged.

"It's that bad, is it?" Maddie asked, her voice growing gentler.

"They aren't the only bodies found in the last forty-eight hours," Carson said. He gazed into his mug, a dark shadow crossing his face. "We found two others just two days ago."

Mike pressed his palms into the table. He hadn't even been aware that anyone else was missing. "Who? How have you kept it a secret?"

"The department has been cautious about this. We don't want to start a panic." Carson took a deep breath. "We believe that the first body we found was Katelyn Harding."

All the air seemed to disappear around Mike. His head spun. Katelyn had gone missing a year ago! How had she been found now? He opened his mouth, wanting to ask, but the words got caught in his throat.

Maddie asked the question that evaded Mike. "You said you found two other bodies."

Carson drained his coffee and pushed back from the table, looking even grimmer than before. "We believe the second body to be Edmund Harding, Katelyn's husband… also killed by a blow to the head."

CHAPTER 3

Maddie stood facing the window; the autumn leaves blew this way and that. A strong wind had ripped several more leaves from the trees, which grew ever more naked. Fall always set a melancholy mood, giving her a languid sense of time. It wasn't precisely depressing, not exactly happy. It was more like a time to stop and think about the year.

Mike and Carson continued to discuss the case behind her. Her hands wrapped around her hot mug of coffee as she listened to them.

"It can't be a coincidence that two couples have been found so recently," Mike said. "How long ago were Katelyn and Edmund killed?"

"I'm still waiting on information about that," Carson replied.

Maddie turned from the window and returned to the table. Only one slice of the quiche was left, but by this time, it seemed her guests were full. She had eaten a small breakfast just before they arrived, so she was pretty full.

"You must have some idea, though," she said as she slid into the chair next to Mike.

Katelyn's disappearance a year ago had hit him very hard then, and she still wasn't entirely sure why. She could only guess that the discovery of her body would affect him now. She gave him a worried look, but he was too focused on Carson to realize it.

The detective hummed as he stretched his back. His eyes were drooping; between that and how he had scarfed down the food, Maddie was sure he wasn't taking care of himself. Of course, that was understandable, given that he was dealing with such a heavy case.

Carson glanced at her, then at Mike, the concern evident on his face.

With a sigh, Mike shook his head. "I know I was a little obsessed with trying to find Katelyn last year, but I'd worked through that. I will not start obsessing about it again... but you have to admit that the cases are similar enough that there's the possibility of a serial killer targeting young couples."

"It's possible," Carson agreed. He spread his hands. "From what it looked like, Katelyn had been killed last year. As for Edmund, he looked as though he'd been killed just a few weeks ago. They were found together, though. Edmund's body had been dumped on top of the place where Katelyn was buried, almost as though someone hoped we'd find her."

"And both were killed by a blow to the head?" Maddie pressed.

Carson nodded.

Maddie considered the situation for a moment, then nodded once to herself. No force on this planet would make her believe Mike was at all connected to these deaths, but she had to know exactly why he was so concerned about Katelyn.

"Let's go to the living room," she suggested. Everyone sitting at the dining table was feeling awkward.

Both men nodded. They moved to the living room, where Carson sat in the recliner and put his feet up. He looked so exhausted that Maddie had to retrieve a fuzzy blanket and tuck it around him. He might be fifteen years older than she and Mike and treat them like one would younger siblings, but sometimes Maddie had motherly urges that she couldn't help but indulge.

Usually, Carson would laugh at her fussing over him. It was a sign of his exhaustion that he took it without comment.

With him taken care of, Maddie sat on the couch and curled her legs under her, turning her focus to Mike. She rested her chin in her hand, considering how to ask the question bouncing around in her mind.

Mike seemed to understand what she needed to know without her asking. He sighed heavily. "I didn't know Katelyn or her husband. It's just that when she went missing, and I saw pictures of her, it reminded me of a missing persons' case from my childhood."

Carson hummed. "Tell us about it if it's not too difficult."

"Well, there isn't much to say... You both know I grew up on a farm. Our school was tiny. Rather than being divided between elementary, middle, and high school, it was all in one building. So I got to know all the teachers very well." Mike paused and straightened the cuffs of his sleeves.

"And... did something happen to one of them?" Maddie pressed.

Mike nodded, not looking at her. "Mrs. Crabtree. She was the kindergarten teacher, and everyone loved her. I liked volunteering in her room because she was so pretty and kind... I was a teenager," he added quickly, looking sheepish. "And though I'm sure my crush was obvious, Mrs. Crabtree ignored it. I felt safe around her."

Maddie smiled softly. She well understood the massive crushes she had on older men when she was a teen as well. Something was alluring about the maturity she was sure they possessed.

"Anyway, I noticed from time to time she had bruises she explained away as being clumsy. But she was the most graceful person I knew." Mike's shoulders were hunched as he let out a heavy breath. "When she went missing, everyone assumed she had run off from her husband."

"Oh," Maddie murmured. Her heart ached for Mike.

He ran a hand through his dark hair. "I knew she hadn't. The day before she went missing, she had promised to bring me some of her Shakespeare collection to borrow. And she left her favorite cardigan in the classroom. I can't tell you why such a simple thing made me so certain... but I knew her husband had killed her."

Carson spoke for the first time in a while. "You can't discount that gut feeling."

"I know that now. But in those days, the police wouldn't listen to me."

Maddie hurried over to Mike's side and put her arms around him. "Did they ever find her?"

Mike nodded slowly. "I did. The family had a golden retriever, and I stole her cardigan. The dog hadn't been trained to track a scent but by some miracle...."

He shrugged, his expression dark.

"And was her husband arrested?" Maddie asked.

"Yes. But it didn't bring her back."

"No wonder Katelyn's disappearance hit you so hard," Maddie rubbed his back. "It brought up that childhood trauma. Especially with so much of the husband's story being that she had just run off for no reason."

Mike nodded.

"Well, we found her now," Carson said. "And no, it doesn't bring her back, but her family will receive some closure. It's an awful thing. Edmund Harding was a terrible bully. When I investigated her disappearance, I heard the most awful things about him."

Surprise washed through Maddie as she looked up at him. "You investigated her case? And didn't tell us?"

Carson smiled wryly as he pushed back the chair, laying a little flatter. "I was strictly forbidden to by the captain. You know how he is."

Maddie wrinkled her nose. She knew that indeed. "Well, I suppose that's a good reason for you not to tell us, then."

"What did you hear?" Mike pushed.

"He was a bully," Carson said. "Not just to his wife, but to everyone. A neighbor had a dog that would bark a few times at night, so Edmund poisoned it. Another neighbor had a collection of gnomes Edmund didn't like, so he drove his truck through her garden beds and destroyed them all."

Maddie gaped. "Why wasn't he arrested for doing those things?"

"Because he had a friend on the force," Carson replied grimly. "A friend who would just make his troubles disappear. When I learned that, I was ready to commit a crime myself... I knew some of my colleagues were corrupt, but I didn't realize it went so... *deep*."

"Was it the captain?" Maddie asked, her eyes widening.

"No. I can't tell you who it is, though… he's still under investigation a year later." Carson shook his head. "But as I was saying. None of the children in the street would dare set foot in his yard since he went after them with a chainsaw one year during Halloween. And I'm not talking about teenagers, either. These were kids under ten."

Mike made a furious noise in his throat. "He seems like a monster! Why would anyone want to scare children like that?"

Maddie folded her arms as she moved back to the couch. It was abundantly clear that Edmund had something to do with Katelyn's death if he would treat strangers like that. "Let me guess… Katelyn tried to leave her just before he killed her."

"Right now, I don't have the evidence to say he killed her," Carson replied, a little strictly. "But… yes."

Maddie closed her eyes. "And the most recent victim… Carla was also trying to leave her husband, wasn't she?"

"She filed for divorce only two days before she went missing."

Maddie's thoughts whirled. Who could be so interested in killing women and their husbands once the couple had separated? Or was it something else? "Women in abusive situations are most likely to be killed when they try to leave."

"They are," Carson agreed.

Mike held up a hand. "But that doesn't explain who killed the husbands if they killed Katelyn and Carla."

Maddie shook her head. "Mike, you and I will go see Carla's parents. Carson, you stay here and have a nap. Understood?"

"I… all right," Carson grumbled. He settled himself deeper in the chair. "But be careful you two. From what I've seen, Carla's father wasn't any better than her husband."

CHAPTER 4

Nobody seemed to be home at the house of Carla's parents. The lawn and flowerbeds, which showed clear signs of being exquisitely cared for, were buried under autumn leaves.

Maddie rang the doorbell again, glancing at Mike. His expression was grim; his forehead furrowed slightly. When he caught Maddie looking at him, he attempted to smooth out his expression. He had a dark theory about what was happening here but hoped he could be proven wrong.

"The car is in the driveway," Maddie said. She knocked loudly on the door. "They have to be home."

"Maybe they went for a walk, or perhaps they have two cars and took one somewhere," Mike said.

But he still didn't believe that was the case. When Maddie peered through one of the side windows, he left the porch and rounded the building.

"Where are you doing?" she asked, following.

"You wait at the door in case someone answers," he told her, waving her back.

Continuing, Mike soon came to a window. He peered inside to find the inside in perfect order. Whoever took care of the house did a thorough job of it. Everything looked like it was out of a magazine rather than a home people lived in.

He knocked at the window and waited. When there was no answer, he rounded the corner and went into the backyard. He found the sliding glass door leading to the back patio ajar.

Mike took a moment to consider his choices. He could get himself, Maddie, and Carson into deep trouble if he went into this house without permission.

On the other hand, if he was right, there was evidence in here that needed to be found, the sooner, the better. And even if Carson came here right then, he'd have to get permission to enter the house. Every minute that passed meant the killer was getting further away.

Mike pulled a handkerchief from his pocket and found a single spot high on the screen door to push it open, careful not to touch anything. "Hello?" he called.

His voice echoed back to him. Hesitating a moment longer, he stepped inside.

Two steps in, and he had a clear view of the kitchen…. And the body that lay on the floor. Mike stopped where he was, his hands clenching at his sides.

He could be alive, he thought, and slowly made his way forward. He stepped into the doorframe leading to the kitchen, and the sight before him made his stomach lurch. Quickly, he retreated to the cool, clean air of the outside.

"Maddie," he called. "Back here—we need Carson."

Carla's mother, Polly, had been killed by a blow to the back of the head. She was lying face-down on the kitchen floor. Based on rigidity and liver temp, the ME guessed she had been dead for over four hours.

Carson stared down at the body grimly. In the space of twenty-four hours, he now had five murders to solve. Even the captain, as much as he disliked Carson's methods, would not stand in his way.

"You really think your two writer friends will help you figure this out?" the captain asked, standing next to Carson in the kitchen, staring down at the body.

"You know I do; you've seen their work," Carson rolled his shoulders. "I need them. The force needs all the help they can get at this point."

"I unfortunately agree. But they are not to interfere with the crime scene, understood?" The captain glared at him until Carson nodded.

A shout came from upstairs, and Carson turned on his heel. He hurried away, the captain hot on his heels. They went into the bedroom as a young sergeant stood in the doorway. Carson recognized her; Adelayne, someone who hadn't been on the force for too long.

This would be her first murder case.

"What is it, Sergeant?" he asked, striding forward.

The captain lagged, silent.

"Sir. There's... well, another body." Adelayne took a deep breath and stepped through the doorway. "Male, mid-seventies by the appearance. Severe damage to the skull."

Carson stepped in. Just as Adelayne said, a second body was on the bed. Make that six, not five, murder victims found in the last forty-eight hours. This man lay on his face, still identifiable despite the damage to his skull.

"You may step outside if you need to, Sergeant," Carson said gently. "Get the ME up here."

The Sergeant nodded once and hurried off. Carson waited half a moment, but it didn't appear the captain was going to join him, so he pulled his tape recorder from his pocket and spoke into it as he observed the room.

"The victim appears to be Gordon Jordanson," he said, "he looks like the man in the pictures around the house. Heavy damage to the skull; at first glance, it appears to have the same damage pattern as the victim downstairs. The room appears untouched. No sign of a struggle."

He stepped around the bed, peering at everything intently. He turned off the recorder, not seeing anything further of note. His brow furrowed. How could someone have their head bashed in like that without putting up a struggle?

The ME came in, and within a few moments, the estimated time of death was the same as the woman downstairs.

Carson thanked him and left the forensic people to do their work while he headed downstairs. Mike and Maddie waited outside on the sidewalk, giving the police room to do their business. The captain was with them.

What is he doing? Carson thought as he headed over.

"Thank you, Captain," Mike said as Carson drew close. "We'll keep that in mind."

The captain looked over them, nodded as though satisfied, and walked off.

Mike and Maddie glanced at one another, rolled their eyes, and faced Carson. Neither of them looked very pleased, but they would have time to talk later about what the captain had said to them.

"Is it true, there's another body?" Maddie said.

"Yes. Another husband and wife, both murdered."

Maddie rocked back on her heels, a thoughtful look on her face. "Another abusive husband and battered wife if what the neighbors say is true. Mike and I talked to a few of them. The neighbor across the street, Sarah, said she heard a great deal of fighting from the house."

"I should talk with her, then," Carson said.

Mike stepped into his path, holding out both hands. "I don't think that's a good idea. As soon as she saw the police arrive, she closed everything up. It seems like she's afraid of talking to the police."

"I see." Carson glanced at the neighboring houses. If he was right, Sarah probably called the police on the loud arguments she'd heard, only for nothing to come of her concerns. He shook his head, glad he had two writer friends to help him get information. "What did she tell you about the couple?"

Maddie nodded at Mike, letting him take the lead. "She said that he was a huge bully. He took great pleasure in harassing the women on the street, so much so that everyone knew not to leave their houses at night."

"She knew him from middle school," Maddie added. "He liked beating up other children and stealing from them."

"So, a bully all his life, then?" Carson surmised.

Mike nodded. "That's what it sounds like."

"And their daughter was killed only hours before they were," Carson continued.

His eyebrows furrowed. He hated this sort of killing, but at least he had some connection to go from. Since four of the victims were related, there might have been a connection between the Hardings and them as we what sort of connection?

"These murders might be less the work of a serial killer and more the work of someone who has a personal motive," he murmured, thinking out loud. "If we can find a connection between all six...."

"I think we should look into the schools they all went to," Maddie said, arms folded over her chest like she was hugging herself. "The insanity of this is scaring me, Carson. But I really do think it has some-thing to do with these men being abusive to their wives."

Carson agreed, but he couldn't figure it out for the life of him. He understood why someone would kill the men, but why would they also kill the women?

He put a hand on each of his young friends' shoulders, looking at them seriously. "I want you both to be extra careful. We've never dealt with a case where our killer was still at large and still killing. Don't let anyone into your homes without identifying them, and for goodness' sake, make sure all your doors and windows are locked—at all times. Understood?"

The last thing he wanted was for either of them to get hurt because of this investigation.

"We will," Maddie promised him. "And you keep yourself safe, too, okay? That includes eating and sleeping."

Carson gave her a fond smile. "Of course, Mother," he teased.

Maddie wrinkled her nose and stuck her tongue out at him.

"In the meantime," Carson continued, "there isn't anything else for you two to do here, and we should wait until we get forensics back before any more theorizing. Go home and get some rest."

Mike nodded. He slid an arm around Maddie's waist, and the two headed toward their vehicle. Carson watched them before he turned back to the house—there were answers; he knew it. He just had to find them.

CHAPTER 5

Mike sat at his old typewriter, staring at the title of the book he had started a year ago and never finished. The plan he'd had for it remained vivid in his mind, yet even now, he couldn't seem to force the words out.

A knock broke through his thoughts, and he jumped. Internally scolding himself for getting startled over such a small thing, he went to the door. Maddie was coming over but remembering Carson's warning, he called through the door.

"Who is it?"

"It's Maddie, and I'm freezing my nose off! Let me in," Maddie answered.

Mike unlocked the door and opened it, welcoming her into his house. She hurried inside, bundled up in her normal sweatpants and oversized jacket. As soon as she was inside, she shed her layers.

"Ahh!" she sighed. "Out of that wind at last."

Mike cocked his head. The howl of an autumn wind outside gave the house a spooky vibe that would be perfect for writing his novel... if he could get into it.

Maddie hung up her outer layers and squinted at him. "Is there a reason you don't have any lights on?"

"Er... just got a lot on my mind, I guess," Mike replied. He turned on a few lights and led Maddie to the living room.

His furniture was a collection of cheap but comfortable things he found at second-hand stores or garage sales. Mike liked luxury in food, but for daily life, it was just a little too much to have fancy sofas. Even the wall art he'd hung around the place were pictures he'd picked up here and there, with no rhyme or reason other than he liked it.

Maddie's eyes fell onto his typewriter, and her eyes lit up. "Are you writing?"

"Not really." Mike closed the typewriter's case and moved it back to the shelf where it belonged. "I thought I would try to get some words out, but I haven't stopped thinking about this case. Not even writing can distract me."

"Oh."

Mike saw the worry in Maddie's eyes, and he winced. The last thing he wanted was to concern her. He smiled. "Don't worry; I'm still eating and sleeping. This isn't going to be like last year."

"I suppose it's been weighing heavy on my mind as well," Maddie said.

It had been three days since they had heard anything new about the case. They had asked around, searching for anything that could help Carson crack this thing. Unfortunately, all they had were theories for the time being.

"Maybe we need to talk about it, then," Maddie said bracingly. "A year ago, we tried to step back and let Carson handle the case and just focus on our own lives. If that will not work, then maybe we should let our imaginations run wild."

Mike laughed at the proposal. If there was anything he could safely say, it was that he and Maddie always let their imaginations run wild.

"They say if you can't beat them, join them," Maddie continued.

"Are you saying you will join me in this obsession because you can't beat it out of me?" Mike teased.

Maddie grinned and nodded. "That and Ben Hiddlestone is coming to town again in a few days. I want the three of us to bash out some good writing times, and we can't do that when we're hung up on this case."

Mike's mood lightened. Since he and Maddie had gotten to know Ben, the three of them had become good friends. He fit nicely into their writing partnership, adding some extra spice to his perspective.

Yes, it would be good to have this whole situation over and done with by the time Ben was here. Not that it was so easy to solve a case. But it gave Mike motivation beyond the obvious. He went to his record player, put on some classical music, and then paced around the living room. Maddie joined him, pumping her arms to get her blood flowing.

"Six people murdered. Three men, three women," Maddie started.

"All killed by a blow to the head," Mike added. "All with cases of domestic violence."

Maddie bumped into him, then stepped around him. "No trace of the killer in any of their homes. Forensic evidence shows the men were all killed by the same baseball bat."

"Unfortunately, baseball bats are difficult to trace, as they are largely made of the same materials."

Maddie hummed. "But the women weren't."

Mike nodded, stepping around Maddie. He faced her and walked backward, hoping it would spark something new in his brain.

"Carla's mother was killed by the same bat, but Carla and Katelyn don't have the same markings," Mike continued. It felt a little silly to repeat the information they already had, but at this point, they needed to find something new in the known. "Katelyn was killed by a blow to the front of the head against something with a sharp angle."

"And Carla has bruises down her side as though she fell down the stairs...." Maddie stopped walking suddenly.

She lifted her hands into the air; one held out to him to stop him from talking while she wrote in the air with her other one. Her lips moved silently as though she was talking to herself. Mike watched, his heart pounding shallowly. Had she figured something out?

"Katelyn's injury," she finally said. "As though she was thrown into the corner of a table or counter."

Mike frowned. "As though she was pushed into it, rather than something hit her head?"

Maddie rushed over to him and positioned themselves both next to the couch. "Pretend that the couch is a table. I'm Katelyn, and you're her husband. You're angry and abusive already and just found out I'm trying to leave you."

"I want you to stay here because I think of you as my property," Mike said.

"I say something that gets you furious—"

"And I hit you," Mike said.

He lifted one hand and mimed a slow punch. Maddie pretended as though he had hit her and stumbled back. She bumped into the couch and pitched forward as she turned to catch her balance. She tapped her head against the back of the couch, then got to the floor.

"Head wounds are deceptive," Mike said as he knelt beside her.

Maddie nodded. "There would be blood everywhere."

"Katelyn's husband might think he killed her, or maybe he would check her pulse and not be able to find it." Mike held his hand to Maddie and helped her back to her feet. "In any case, he doesn't want to call for help. His friend on the police force can only do so much."

"And covering up a murder isn't something he'd do," Maddie finished.

Mike shook his head, his eyes blazing. "And so he ditches Katelyn's body and reports her as missing. He plays the worried, grieving husband all the while knowing she's dead... and never has to face the consequences of his actions."

"Precisely," Maddie said.

"And Carla?"

Maddie positioned them both in front of the sofa again. "You're Carla, and I'm the husband. I'm angry because I just found out you're trying to leave me. We're standing in front of the stairs. I push you; I know that it'll hurt, but I also know that you won't dare tell anyone."

She lifted her hands and pantomimed a shove at his chest, not actually touching him.

Mike fell back, stiffening his body slightly, so his head hit the cushioned back of the couch. He imagined landing in such a way against a flight of stairs and winced.

"And again, it's a head injury. The blow killed her, so the husband, panicking, disposes of her body." Maddie paced again, her hands clasped behind her back. "Only someone had to know. Someone saw that Katelyn had been killed by a blow to the head and decided to kill her husband the same way."

"And then went after Carla's husband after it became clear that he killed his wife, as well," Mike murmured. "But why Carla's parents?"

Maddie tapped her lips with one finger. "Because they knew? Maybe because they told him where to find her after she tried to leave him?"

Mike hummed as he crossed his legs. "Her father was abusive toward her mother. A man like that wouldn't care so much that his daughter was being abused."

"And the mother could think that, since she put up with it, her daughter should as well. Maybe they taught Carla that it was her own doing, that she deserved it somehow." Maddie shivered. "That doesn't get us any closer on who would care so much about these women that they'd kill to avenge them, though."

"Yeah. It doesn't seem like Katelyn or Carla had friends. So who?" Mike stood again and went to the record player.

As he watched the record wind itself slowly in a circle, he thought back to when he was a teenager, and Mrs. Crabtree had gone missing. In his young mind, he had been confident that if her husband had been brought to justice, it would make him feel better about her death somehow…

Of course, it hadn't. The only thing that helped was time and learning to stop blaming himself.

"But what if our killer couldn't do that?" he said aloud, though he knew Maddie wouldn't understand what he was talking about. "What if the killer blames themselves for Katelyn and Carla's deaths?"

CHAPTER 6

When Carson arrived at Mike's house early the following day, he found not one but two big corkboards sitting propped against the couch with dozens of newspaper clippings and articles printed from the internet pinned on them.

"I see you have been busy," he noted.

"The killer's name is Donovan Collins," Mike declared.

Carson's eyebrows rose. He had seen his young writer friends be confident with their deductions before… but had never had so much reason to doubt them.

The whole place was a wreck, unlike the meticulous Mike. Maddie sat perched on the back of a chair, pounding down a Red Bull while several other energy drinks lay on the surrounding floor. The table was covered with several meals' worth of takeout that had been eaten.

He frowned in worry at them. Maddie and Mike were slightly bloodshot, the sort of red-eyed look they got when they ended up staying up all night writing.

"Put that down," he said sharply when Maddie picked up another energy drink.

She dropped it, looking startled.

"We figured it out," Mike said. "Don't worry about the mess; I'll clean it up after I sleep."

Carson folded his arms. "You've both been up all night?"

Maddie and Mike glanced at one another, looking startled. It was as though neither of them realized what time it was. Carson rubbed his forehead.

"Maddie, get down from there. Both of you sit down and start trying to relax while you tell me what you figured out," Carson ordered.

Obediently, Mike sank into an armchair, and Maddie clambered down from her perch. She slumped back and yawned. Carson ensured they had no secret energy drinks around them and cleaned up the mess.

"All right. So, you think it's Donovan Collins," Carson said, monitoring them. He swept the empty food containers into a large black garbage bag. "Why would you think that?"

Mike straightened up some. "Twenty years ago, Donovan Collins was a twelve-year-old boy. His abusive father murdered his mother; the evidence was all there, and Donovan testified against his father, but for some reason, he was never convicted."

"Online rumor has it that Collins senior paid off the judge or perhaps blackmailed him," Maddie explained. "Anyway, the case was thrown out of court, and he was never brought to justice for killing his wife."

Mike nodded; his hands were clenched on his knees. "He was only a child, but the trauma of seeing his father kill his mother never left him. His father ended up locking him away in a psychiatric hospital...."

"Except he died two years ago," Maddie said.

Carson tied off the bag. "How could he have killed our victims if he died?"

"The father died, not the son. Donovan is still alive. But with his father's death, he no longer had the money to keep his room at the hospital and was released." Maddie nodded as though that explained it.

Mike cleared his throat. "Katelyn worked at the hospital. She would have become like a second mother to him. And when she went missing, he would have thought of his own mother, just like I thought of Mrs. Crabtree."

Carson finally finished his cleaning and came to look at the corkboards. Every article had to do with the women's deaths; he frowned as he saw several printouts from online chat rooms.

"What's this?" he asked, pointing.

"We tracked down Donovan's various online presences," Maddie replied. "Since he spent so much of his life with his internet usage controlled, he didn't know how to protect his online identity. It was easy."

Mike stood and pulled one of the chat records off the board. "See this? He was researching ways to find a dead body. He claimed to be a writer and joined several writer's groups to ask."

"I've researched far more suspicious things," Maddie added. "Sometimes, as writers, we get into too much detail on this sort of thing."

Carson nodded once—he agreed with that statement.

"Anyway, Donovan was brutally abused by his father and saw his mother in these murdered women," Mike continued. "His experiences told him that the police wouldn't do anything, even if they had the evidence to convict their husbands."

"That isn't evidence."

Mike shook his head. "Read this. Just read it! It contains the exact details of these deaths. He got close to the husbands, found out what they did, and as soon as he was convinced that they had killed their wives, he killed them."

Maddie joined them. "Carla's parents remained in contact with her husband, even after she left him. I'm sure the phone records will show that they called him; they must have told him where to find her, and he abducted her."

"Abducted?"

"Yes. That's why she was in that getup, why there were bruises on her wrists." Maddie showed him another article. "Her husband wanted to control her and was keeping her a prisoner... perhaps even in her own parents' home. She must have tried to escape, and he pushed her down the stairs, killing her."

"So Donovan killed them, too, blaming them for Carla's death," Mike completed with a flourish.

Carson whistled through his teeth. "It's not evidence."

"No, it's not," Mike agreed. "But it's enough for you to find the evidence that you need."

It was a lead; that was right. More of a lead than Carson had had so far. He gathered the clippings and printings off the boards.

"Thank you," he said. "I'll take this to the captain. It might be enough for a search warrant. If Donovan Collins did kill those people, we'll find some evidence."

"The baseball bat," Maddie told him. "He was in Little Leagues when his mother was killed. He used that bat. He'll have kept it… for the next time."

Carson thanked them grimly. With any luck, they were right. And if they were, then he might prevent even more murders.

EPILOGUE

A month later, Mike carried a full manuscript of a new novel within a binder tucked under his arm. The autumn leaves crunched underfoot as he walked up the drive to a rather large home. A dog barked behind the fence, that eager, joyful bark of a dog finding a new friend.

"Hello, Copper," he called as he stepped onto the porch.

Tricia answered the door almost before he rang the bell. She beamed at him, dressed in a blue apron. Flour dusted in her hair. "Come on in. The cookies are almost finished."

Mike entered the house. He'd been sure to take allergy medication before coming here to tolerate Copper's dander.

"Is that the book?" Tricia asked eagerly, eyeing the package under his arm.

"Yep," Mike replied. He followed Tricia into the kitchen. "Autumn Leaves. A Halloween story of mystery, danger, and paranormal thrills."

Since they had met that day, Mike and Tricia had become close friends. He enjoyed having another person to spend time with, and she had seamlessly entered the group with Maddie, Carson, and Ben Hiddlestone.

Game nights were exhilarating these days, as Tricia and Ben had competitive streaks that none of the others had.

She also had a tremendous love for horror, a genre Mike had little experience with that Maddie refused to read. Tricia would be invaluable as the first eyes to read his new novel.

Her kitchen was a disaster zone of flour, sugar, and baking supplies. Mike kept the edges so as not to dirty his clothes as he watched her finish plopping the cookie dough onto a baking sheet.

"I heard that the Collins trial was finished today," Tricia said, glancing at him. "That poor man... I couldn't bear to turn on the news and see if he was convicted."

Mike put his hands in his pockets. "He was found not responsible for his actions. He'll be treated in a psychiatric hospital for the rest of his life."

Tricia sighed. "I hope he finds some peace."

"As do I." Mike considered the case. It had been the most sobering one he'd ever been involved in... and yet, he felt lighter than he had in years. "Maddie and I plan to visit him from time to time. Hopefully, having people who care about him will help."

Tricia smiled at him as she put the cookies in the oven. "You're a good man, Mike."

"I certainly try to be." He beamed at her.

She blushed slightly, then wiped the flour off her hand. "Now. While those cook, let's have a look at this novel, shall we?"

Mike grinned. "Of course! Let's begin."

The End

THE CASE OF THE MISSING COFFIN

AN ANNIE ARCHER PARANORMAL
MYSTERY

CHAPTER 1

I t wasn't often that Annie wished there were more ghosts in attendance. Even for a witch, there was something a little unnerving about spirits hanging around when they should be moving on. Not that Annie knew precisely where they 'moved on' to. She had heard several theories over the years. It wasn't just non-witches that lacked insight into the afterlife.

Today, though, she kept scanning the gathered mourners, searching for any sign that the deceased's spirit lingered.

It would be a comfort to her family, Annie thought.

A shiver ran down her spine. Even though she had gotten involved in several murder cases since she moved to this small town, this was the worst. Her heart ached for Isabella Turner, the young shining star on her way to becoming a world-famous pianist.

Now she was in a closed casket.

Annie scanned the crowd one last time. No spirits, but she spied her friend, Detective Adam Parker. Adam caught her eye, and Annie flushed. She spun her face back, hoping he hadn't thought she was looking for him.

Only a few minutes later, Adam was next to her. He touched her wrist, and when she glanced at him, she found he was frowning with a soft look in his eyes.

"Are you okay?" he asked in a whisper.

Annie nodded. "We can talk later."

Adam nodded once. He remained where he was next to her, his fingers brushing against her wrist. On a frosty morning, the warmth of his touch made her relax a little. She turned her attention back to the minister as he finished his sermon. As Isabella was lowered to the ground, a single sob broke the solemn air.

A flicker caught Annie's eye, but when she turned her head, hoping to see Isabella's spirit, the movement was gone.

Shortly after, the family moved back toward their cars. Annie and Adam hung back, waiting for the rest of the mourners to follow them before they took up the end of the line. As they made their way toward the parking lot, Annie's heart was heavy.

"Are you okay?" Adam asked again.

Annie sighed. "Yes. I just wish I had found her, you know? I couldn't get a single vision in all the potions and spells I used. I talked to my mentor, Rosemary. She has no idea why I even started having the visions, let alone why they stopped."

Her arms tightened around herself. She hated feeling as somber as she did at this moment. Usually, she was lighthearted even in the face of hardship. She hadn't felt this way since her divorce.

Adam nodded slowly. "I understand what you mean."

Annie reached for his hand this time. Her heart ached not only for Isabella's family but also for Adam. He was the one who had found Isabella.... Only too late. He'd tracked down her abductor, Jonathan Swift, and found Isabella dead.

"If I had been half an hour earlier, she might have had a chance," Adam whispered.

"And if I had been able to tap into those visions, I could have helped you find her half an hour earlier," Annie said miserably.

Adam came to a stop. They turned to each other, and Annie's breath caught in her throat. She had never seen the detective look at her this way before. His eyes smoldered, but she couldn't tell what emotion he was feeling.

"It's not your fault," he said. "And it's not my fault, as hard as it is for us to accept that. The fault lies with Jonathan Swift, and he will get his punishment for this crime."

"Want to come to my house?" Annie asked impulsively. "I baked some dinner for the Turner family and delivered it."

She didn't add that she was going to bake a spell to help comfort them in their grief. Despite the popular notion of witches, Annie considered herself a 'good witch.' Honestly, she felt the vast majority of witches were good, but there were some bad ones out there. Just a few months ago, one such wicked witch attempted to murder the town's mayor.

Most witches kept to themselves and tried not to use their magic very often. However, Annie had decided at a young age that she wanted to help people. Using her special talents was the best way she could see to do that.

Adam ran a hand through his hair. "I would like that. I don't like the idea of returning to the office; my home is just so empty. And maybe I could have one of your special teas, too."

Was he asking for a spell? Annie was surprised to hear that. Adam rarely liked to meddle with the supernatural. He'd accept her visions as help in his cases, but that was about it.

"Want to take my car?" Annie asked, arching a brow at him.

Adam nodded. "I can come back later to get mine."

Annie changed her direction slightly, heading for the bubble-gum pink Volkswagen beetle at the far end of the parking lot. As they walked, Annie glanced around the cemetery before she sighed.

"Who are you looking for?"

"I… was hoping to see something I could use to comfort the family," Annie hedged. "From everything I have heard, Isabella was a beautiful woman with a kind and generous heart to match. I can't imagine the pain they are going through right now."

Adam's gaze darkened.

"Sorry," Annie whispered.

They continued in silence. Isabella Turner had been much loved in the community before she was abducted. It was easy to see why Jonathan Swift had targeted her. It just made Annie sick to her stomach, thinking that the man had been so obsessed with finding the rein-carnation of his late wife that he targeted young women born the day she died.

Even though the trial was still ongoing, everyone was sure Jonathon would face the full punishment he could for murder. The transcripts Annie saw of the interrogation were blood-chilling. It was clear from how he spoke that Isabella wasn't his first victim.

He had abducted women before and, upon discovering that they weren't the reincarnation of his wife, he killed them, calling them 'imposters' as though any of them had claimed to be whom he was looking for.

Once they were at her car, Adam stopped with a distracted look on his face.

"Adam?"

He jumped. "Oh. Sorry. Just thinking."

Annie took his hand in hers, concerned. He wasn't acting like himself, either. "Tell me."

Adam stared at her for a long moment, a look of shock on his face. Annie wasn't sure why, but she tightened her hold on him. She kept focused on his eyes, watching as he turned over his thoughts in his mind.

Eventually, he ran his hand through his hair again. "The last time I interviewed him, Swift showed there were five other women he killed, but I haven't gotten their names. I can't help but keep thinking that I need to find them. As heartbreaking as it is for the families, they deserve to know what happened to their daughters."

Annie swallowed hard. She wanted so badly to volunteer her help, but the visions she had grown used to had halted. Her mentor once suggested that she had been drugged, which was why the visions started in the first place.

Was there a way to trigger them again?

"That's why I came here," Adam said. He slid into the passenger's seat of the beetle.

Annie quickly rounded the car and got into the driver's side. She turned it on; it purred to life, instantly pouring hot air. She sighed in relief as she held her icy fingers in front of the flow. The spell she had developed to work on cars to make them run more efficiently had worked.

"You think someone here had something to do with Jonathan Swift?" she asked.

Adam shook his head. "Not directly. I hope something will come up; maybe they will think of something. Most people don't realize how important even small clues are. Anything will help."

Annie pulled out of the parking stall and took up a spot at the end of the line. The cars were moving slowly away from the cemetery.

"I might have a way to help," she offered hesitantly.

"Are you having visions again?"

"No. But I could put together an importance spell… it might help the family remember any important details they have missed or blocked out. Or I could try a seance and contact the dead women." Her voice betrayed how much she doubted that would help.

Adam shook his head. "If I find nothing soon, I might turn to your magic. Right now, though, I hope Swift gives up the locations he buried them voluntarily."

Annie nodded once as they got to the turnoff onto the road. While most of the cars turned left, she took the right turn. "Of course. I guess I could give him a truth potion, too. I just have this awful feeling that something's not quite adding up, Adam. And I don't know why."

"Me, too," Adam's expression grew troubled, and he turned his face out the window. "Maybe it's the weather."

"Maybe," Annie agreed.

But she knew it wasn't.

CHAPTER 2

Adam and Annie drove quietly to her house on the outskirts of town. It was a small cottage with a small yard. Annie had been planning to start a window box herb garden for some time, but life always seemed too busy for her.

Her ghostly roommate, Monty, paced around the front hall, his hands clasped behind his back when Annie unlocked the door. He looked up, and the pale, almost translucent expression turned from worry to relief. Annie gave him a reassuring smile.

Where have you been? He signed. The gash across his neck made it impossible for him to communicate any other way.

It had been a long, painstaking process for both of them to learn ASL, but at least they could have some sort of conversation now.

Adam entered the cottage behind Annie; his head bowed as though deep in thought. Upon seeing him, Monty scowled and narrowed his eyes at Annie. *You were with him?*

Annie sighed. She knew better than to think Monty was jealous, but since they had been able to talk to each other, he had become rather possessive of her time. "Let's go to the kitchen," she said aloud, "the funeral was rather draining."

Monty's scowl deepened. His form flitted out of vision, but when

Annie led Adam into the kitchen, he was waiting for them. The dead rarely seemed to be too interested in the goings-on of the living; if anything, they were curious or annoyed at the interruptions. Annie wondered if Monty had witnessed his funeral.

"Do you know who the other women Jonathan Swift killed are?" Annie asked as she went to start the kettle.

Adam slumped into a chair near the table. "There are a few possibilities, but without finding them or Swift telling us who they were, there's no actual way of knowing."

"Maybe if we found a connection between any of them and Isabella, we'd have a chance," Annie mused. She prepared the teapot with a spell-infused lavender tea. It would help them relax and hopefully clear away the cobwebs from their minds.

Adam ran a hand through his hair. "I have seen nothing. Maybe you could look through their files and see if I missed something."

"If nothing else, I'd see what they looked like. It might help with the dreams."

Adam nodded once.

The kettle started whistling, and Annie took it off the heat. "I really hoped that her spirit would be at the funeral. I can't imagine how much the family is going through."

Monty rolled his eyes as he walked back and forth, passing through Adam repeatedly.

It's like living with a cat, Annie thought.

"Her spirit?" Adam frowned at her as she poured out the tea. "Wait, were you serious about the seance?"

Monty looked alarmed. *Not in my house, you don't!*

Annie ignored Monty instead of answering Adam. "I thought about it. She might give us more information. Like if Swift was working with someone else."

"There's no evidence to show he was."

"Then perhaps if I could contact his actual wife, I could get him to—"

Adam held up a hand to stop her. His eyes were slightly narrowed, and his lips pressed into a thin line. "For starters, you aren't going anywhere near that man. I know you can take care of yourself in most circumstances, but I don't want him to so much as look at you."

Annie set the tea in front of him, startled at this display of protectiveness. She opened her mouth to ask about it but quickly shut it again. His protectiveness wasn't because of the spark between them... was it?

"All right, but I could give you information to share with him to make him spill his guts," she said, fighting to keep her cool.

"Annie... No seances. I don't believe in all that crap. Spirits, ghosts, what have you." Adam wrapped his hands around the mug of tea and stared into it with a stern expression.

Monty, who was now standing behind Adam, looked affronted. His mouth and hands both moved rapidly as though he was trying to shout at Adam. Of course, Adam had no idea that Monty was even there.

"So you believe in my magic but not in ghosts?" Annie asked carefully. He believed in her magic, didn't he?

"Of course, I believe in *your* magic, Little Witch," Adam said. He offered her a smile, but it didn't reach his eyes. "But all this other stuff? I have to draw a line somewhere."

Annie sipped her tea. The floral flavor filled her mouth as the spell started working at once, relaxing her tense muscles. She shook her head. "Then I guess if I were to tell you I have a ghost for a roommate, and he's standing right behind you, you wouldn't believe me?"

Adam straightened. He turned, and Monty gestured rudely at him. When Adam turned back, though, he was frowning. "Don't make fun of me. I can't take it today."

"I'm not making fun of you. But ghosts are real, and I have a ghost roommate."

Adam turned the mug around in his hands. "Are you safe here?"

Monty threw his hands into the air and disappeared.

"Of course. Most ghosts want to be left alone," Annie assured him. "Although Monty seems to be pretty disgusted with you right now."

Adam turned again. "I'm sorry for offending you."

Annie couldn't help but laugh. "Oh, so you believe me?"

"I will not call you a liar. But, still, I wouldn't say I like the idea of a seance or anything that will put you in contact with Swift's wife. He could decide that means you're her reincarnation."

"I'm too old to be her reincarnation."

"Annie, the man's delusional. I don't care if he's in prison; there's still a slight chance that he could get out again one way or another. And if he thinks you're connected to his wife...." Adam took a large swallow of the tea. He winced as the hot liquid seared down his throat.

Annie nodded once. "Okay. I won't. So, what do we do now?"

"The Turner family is hosting a wake tonight. We could see if we can find out any information. If that doesn't work, then your baked spells." Adam's expression changed briefly, as though he wanted to add something, but he only drank more tea.

"Adam..." Annie hesitated.

Adam looked at her curiously, and a strange longing swept through her. She wanted nothing more than to help him figure this out. She reached across the table to take his hand. "We'll find them. I know we will."

"Thank you," Adam whispered. "You don't know how much that means to me."

He squeezed her fingers, the warmth of the tea lingering on his palm. Annie's heart skipped a beat, but Monty appeared behind Adam before she could repeat anything. He pointed at the doorway, scowling.

"Come on," Annie said as she stood. "We should get to the wake."

Adam nodded, looking like he would rather be anywhere else. Annie had to wonder why this case was hitting him so much harder than the ones they had worked on in the past. She didn't want to pry, though, at least not until they had found the missing women.

The wake was being held in the reception hall at the nicest hotel in town. Everything was curtained in a somber black, and at the front of the room was a memorial display of Isabella.

As Annie and Adam entered, she spotted someone lingering near the display. They were dressed in a long black coat, and from behind, she couldn't tell what gender they were. The person's head was bowed, one hand reaching out to touch the nearest picture of Isabella. They turned slightly, looking at Isabella's parents, then abruptly spun on their heels. They disappeared through a side door.

That was suspicious, Annie thought.

But the Turners were approaching her and Adam now. She pulled her mind from the figure, promising to tell Adam about it when they had the chance.

"Mr. and Mrs. Turner," Adam greeted them with a polite nod when they stopped in front of him. "I came to pay my respects."

Mrs. Turner pulled him into a hug. "Thank you, Detective."

Adam patted the woman's back. "I... I don't feel like I deserve your thanks."

"You do," Mr. Turner said. "If it weren't for you, we never would have gotten her back. She has a proper burial now, and I hope she's found peace."

Annie stepped forward now. "Mr. Turner, Mrs. Turner. My name is Annie. I sometimes help Detective Parker with his cases. I am very sorry for your loss. Even though I didn't know her personally, I felt the positive impact she had on the community."

The Turners both gave her watery smiles. Mr. Turner pulled Adam aside, murmuring he wanted to ask something. Annie watched them go, a knotted sensation in her stomach.

"You said you work with the detective?" Mrs. Turner asked timidly, breaking the silence.

Annie turned back to her. "Yes."

"Then you know... Isabella might not have been the first woman killed by that monster." Mrs. Turner searched her expression.

Annie winced. "I... can't comment at this time."

Mrs. Turner took hold of her wrist. "It's all right. I'm not asking for details like my husband. I want a promise from you. Find those other girls. Their parents deserve to give them a proper burial."

"We will do the best we can," Annie promised her. She glanced over at Adam, whose expression was torn between sorrow and sympathy. Determination welled in her. *And we will use every means we can as well.*

CHAPTER 3

When someone tapped her shoulder, Annie was at the local plant nursery, hoping to find the ingredients she needed for some potions. She nearly jumped out of her skin and whirled. Her heart thudding jumped up another notch when she saw who it was—Adam.

Clearing her throat, she swatted his arm. "What are you doing, sneaking up on me like that?"

"Sorry." Adam held his hands in surrender, but an impish smile crossed his face. "You looked so lost in thought that I decided to see if you were Astro-projecting.

Annie was so happy to see that the heavy cloud smothering him at the funeral had lifted. She rolled her eyes at him but smiled in return. It had been a couple of days since they last talked. Adam was busy investigating the physical leads and continuing to interrogate Jonathan Swift while Annie looked more into her visions and how to get them back.

"I was heading to your house when I saw your car out front." Adam nodded toward the exit of the store.

"You were? Why didn't you call me?"

"I did, several times. It's why I was heading over there. I was worried about you."

Annie pulled her cell phone from her pocket and grimaced. "Sorry, I forgot to charge it last night; I've been scattered these last couple of days."

Adam nodded. They started down the aisle again. Annie breathed in the rich scent of earth and fresh greenery. She paused at a chocolate mint plant and picked it up. The potent scent hit her in the back of the throat, creating a pleasant coolness.

"These things are amazing," she told Adam, showing him the label. "They have such a powerful flavor. All you need to do is suck on one leaf, and it lasts. Better than chewing gum."

"I'm not overly fond of chocolate and mint together."

Annie laughed. "It doesn't really taste like chocolate." She put the plant into her basket. "See if you can find some hibiscus and stinging nettles, will you?"

Adam's brow scrunched. "I never thought you'd use such common plants in a witches' brew."

"There's more to potions than just these plants. You could put together something exactly as I do, but without the spells, it's just a delicate tea." Annie picked up a thyme plant and sniffed its leaves. It smelled a little dusty and old, so she put it back. "I talked with Rosemary a few times since we last saw watch other."

"Did she give you any help?"

"She gave me some hints about maybe jumpstarting the visions again. She suggested that something personal is holding me back from connecting with the lives of the women we're looking for."

"It's not a seance?" Adam asked.

Annie frowned at him. "Why are you so hung up on that? Seances are perfectly normal. Many cultures call on their ancestors for help, and a seance is one way of doing it. It's not all hokey chants and fake mumbo jumbo."

"I didn't mean it like that. I just... don't want you to get yourself in trouble, okay?" Adam's cheeks flushed as he grabbed a strawberry plant. He turned it around in his hands before holding it up. "You know, you have some magnificent property. You could probably grow a bunch of this yourself. I could build you some raised garden boxes if you want."

Annie wasn't sure how to answer that. She wondered if he was changing the subject or making the offer for another reason. "Uh, sure. That would be great. I've been meaning to put in a garden, but with all the cases we've had, I guess I haven't taken the time."

"We'll figure out a time for that, then. In the meantime, would you like to join me in interviewing the families of the missing women? I've narrowed the potential victims to five whom I believe are certainly Swift's victims." Adam put the strawberry plant back.

Annie considered it as she moved down the next row, then shook her head sadly. "I don't think it will do any good. I'm not good at reading people, and Rosemary says I need to eliminate distractions. So that's what I'm doing."

She wouldn't admit it, but there was more than just hearing the victims' families and seeing their grief that would distract her. It was happening more and more that Adam would intrude on her thoughts. His kind smile, sparkling eyes, and teasing lilt to his voice. She'd always found him attractive, but something was getting stronger these days.

Shaking her head, she resumed her search. "I can't let myself be distracted. You follow the evidence. I'll bring the magic."

⁕

It was nighttime before the potions were ready. She had prepared a concentration brew, a relaxation brew, a mind-clearing potion, and then five connection potions. There was one connection potion for each of the women who had disappeared. She had the names and faces of the ones Adam thought Swift had also killed.

Despite her potions, Annie still felt a distant sort of anxiety. If the potions worked and connected her to the murdered women, she would, at best, witness their deaths. At worst, she would live through them.

Don't let yourself be distracted; she reminded herself. Her inner voice sounded oddly like Rosemary's.

Thinking about her mentor released some of the tension she carried.

Centering herself once more, Annie picked up the first missing person's report. It was the most recent of the missing women... the most likely to be found alive, however unlikely it was.

Monty had been nowhere to be found all day, and Annie was grateful for the solitude. Her candles were lit in a circle around her, lighting her surroundings as she opened the file. Yasmine Delisle. She was married with two children. She volunteered at soup kitchens, and her disappearance was initially thought to be connected to a recent rash of drug-related crime in the area.

Her husband still lived in the apartment Yasmine's parents had gifted the newlyweds for their wedding in Chicago. He worked from home part-time as an editor while taking care of their children. The two of them were, by all accounts, happily married. He offered a reward for any information linked to her disappearance.

Annie turned the page and read the details of her abduction. She was an elementary school teacher and left work one day to deal with a problem at the soup kitchen where she volunteered. She never made it to the kitchen and never returned to work. Her journals spoke of some dissatisfaction with her current situation but were full of love for her husband and children. No sign she was planning to leave. No indication that she was afraid for her life.

The last person to have seen her alive was one of her seven-year-old students, except for her abductor.

"I'm sorry for your pain, Yasmine," Annie said out loud. Rosemary told her it might help to talk to the person she was trying to find as though they were in the room with them. "You must be so worried about your husband and children. I want to help you. I want you to find peace."

Annie lapsed into silence. What more could she say? She slid the photograph of Yasmine out and set the file aside. Then, she reached into another file and found Jonathan Swift's mugshot. As she looked at his picture, a shudder ran down her spine. He looked like a completely normal person. Average. Not very attractive, but not unattractive, either.

Something in his eyes made her senses rub raw, though. Or maybe it was only because she knew what he was capable of.

"You, I don't want to connect to," she told the photo. "But if it means finding Yasmine and the other women, I will. You are a terrible person. I will find them, though. You can't stop me."

She set the two pictures down side by side and picked up her first connection potion. She put it on the floor between the pictures and dipped her fingers into it. Sprinkling the potion on the two photos, she murmured spells under her breath. Finally, she picked up Yasmine's picture and put it on fire with a lighter. As flames licked up the side of the photo, Annie caught the ash in her potion.

Once the fire consumed the picture, she drank the potion and lay on the floor. The light from the candles seemed to sway on either side of her as she stared up and concentrated on the mental image of Yasmine's face.

"You shouldn't be here."

Annie's eyes snapped open. She bolted upright, gasping in surprise. This wasn't in her bedroom. She sat on a sidewalk, but the world around her seemed hazy. It shifted and pulled around her. Annie scrambled to her feet, looking around.

She gasped when she saw the woman standing next to her. "Yasmine?"

Yasmine stared at her. "You shouldn't be here."

"Where is here?" Annie asked, looking around.

"Chicago. I'm trying to find my home, but I'm stuck here." Yasmine pointed toward a house labeled 4738.

"Is this where he took you?"

"Who?"

"Jonathan Swift."

Yasmine only kept staring at the house without a reaction. "I tried to be a good wife—a good mother. I tried. But I felt like I was failing at every turn. I wish I could see them one last time. I want... tell my husband I'm not in pain."

Annie rubbed her arms. It was only now that she realized how cold she was. When she looked down at herself, she saw a thin layer of frost building on her skin. Her breath puffed out in a misty cloud.

"Tell them," Yasmine murmured, but her voice seemed to come from far away. "Promise me."

Annie fell to her knees, too cold to stand. She felt her eyes freeze over and screamed, her voice echoing in the shifting world as it tore her throat.

CHAPTER 4

Annie's back bent, pain shooting through her as she screamed. She bolted upright, finding herself on her bedroom floor once more. The candles she'd lit the previous night were nothing more than puddles of wax now; each one melted out and then hardened again. The curtains, closed the previous night, were pulled apart, and the window was open.

"What?" Annie murmured. Her throat was raw and hurt as she got to her feet.

Her legs wobbled, and she sat back down. Now that she was growing more aware of herself, she was full of aches and pains, as though she had been beating herself against the floor. The time she had spent in the dream was so short, yet hours had gone by.

A tiny scraping sound made her glance to her left. Monty sat on the floor, scraping his fingernails on the floor. Once he got her attention, he pointed at her and signed so rapidly that Annie couldn't keep up with his admonishing.

"Did you open the window?" Annie asked, attempting to stand again. She was freezing!

Monty scowled but nodded.

Interesting. When she first got to the cottage, Annie had to put a spell on the remote so Monty could watch TV and not get so bored. He was getting more proficient in interacting with the world of the living without the spells.

"I didn't think you cared," Annie teased over her shoulder as she reached the window. She slid them shut and then sat back on her bed.

When she glanced at Monty, his scowl was even deeper. *I don't want any newbies moving into the home. You're barely tolerable as it is.*

Annie couldn't help but laugh. Her head throbbed, though, so she groaned as she lay back. "I'm fine. I need a little rest to get over it. Thank you, Monty."

No response. But Monty was gone when she glanced at where he had been sitting. Annie smiled to herself as she pulled a blanket up to her chin and let her eyes flutter shut. Living with him really was like living with a cat, she mused. He acted all aloof and like he didn't care, but when it came down to it, he did.

Annie slept for another three hours, but when she woke the second time, the aches and pains were gone. She felt alert and full of energy.

Remembering how her inability to answer her phone yesterday worried Adam, the first thing she did was check to see if she had missed any messages. Nothing. She wasn't sure if she was disappointed or not by that.

"No time to dwell on that," she told herself briskly as she jumped out of bed.

Within a few minutes, she was in her car, driving to the police station. The details of her vision remained crisp in her mind as she found a parking spot and headed in. The officers were used to seeing her consult with Adam, so they nodded to her in greeting as she made her way to the office that had 'Detective Parker' written on it.

Annie didn't even think about knocking before she breezed in. "We're going on a road trip," she declared.

Adam sat at his desk. His usually unruffled appearance was disheveled. Pictures and files lay on his desk in an organized grid pattern, and he held a half-empty cup of coffee. Five o'clock shadow was starting to darken his chin and cheeks.

"What are you talking about?" he asked, sounding exhausted.

"Have you been awake all night?" Annie asked in worry. She closed the office door.

Adam grunted, looking a little embarrassed. "Not entirely. But I don't have the brainpower to be productive."

"I'll drive, and you can have a nap. I'll also buy you breakfast and fresh coffee when we get there," Annie decided.

"Where?" Adam asked. An edge of irritation entered his voice.

Annie shook her head, grimacing. Right. She had forgotten entirely that he didn't know everything she did. "I performed a ritual last night—"

Adam straightened, an alarmed look on his face.

"I didn't call on the dead at all," she said quickly, even though that wasn't entirely true. He didn't need to know all the details. "I was able to force a vision last night, and I could see some things. I think I know where Yasmine Delisle is."

Adam put down his coffee and stood, grabbing his suit jacket off the back of his chair. "You saw where she's buried?"

Annie let out a shuddering breath. "Not exactly. I don't think Swift buried her... at least, not yet. So, let's go; I don't want to leave her there any longer than we already have."

Something flitted across Adam's expression, but he only nodded once as he gestured for her to lead the way out of the office.

It took them a little over five hours to get to Chicago. Adam fell asleep before they even hit the highway, and though Annie wanted to tell him everything she had discovered, she also wanted to let him rest. He looked so exhausted.

In the end, she put a spell over his area of the car to keep from hearing the noise, then put on some upbeat music to keep her awake. He woke up naturally just before they reached the city, and Annie turned off the music before she removed the surrounding spell.

"Need some breakfast and coffee?" she asked brightly.

Adam rubbed his eyes. "That would be great—my treat, okay?"

"Sure thing."

"I can't believe how hard I slept. Guess this beetle isn't as uncomfortable as I feared." He gave her a bit of a lopsided grin before he settled back in the seat. "So, are you going to tell me what happened now?"

Annie hesitated. She wasn't entirely sure how to describe what had happened to her the previous night. She certainly didn't want to tell Adam—she didn't want him to worry about her. So, she finally just shrugged. "I induced another vision and found a house where I believe Yasmine's body is. First, though, we have to find a funeral home."

Adam frowned. "Funeral home?"

"Meadowlark Funerals and Caskets," Annie rambled off, rolling her shoulders. The long drive had left her muscles tight and sore again.

"That sounds familiar... isn't that the funeral home Jonathan Swift went through for his wife's funeral?" Adam's jaw tightened visibly, and Annie could see that he was upset by this news. "I should have investigated them. They're connected to the killings?"

Annie sorted through the details of her vision again. She had seen the sign for the funeral home, but unlike 4738, she hadn't felt a sense of dread about it. If anything, the funeral home provided a sense of peace. She wasn't sure what to expect there.

"I think it will give us answers," she finally said.

After getting some food, they headed to the funeral home. A faint mist hung in the air despite it being mid-afternoon. Brick buildings lined the streets, and in the shimmering light, it looked like they had stepped back in time. The sidewalks were empty, and other than a few birds sitting on the roofs of the stores, it looked utterly deserted.

"It's kind of spooky," Adam noted as they headed toward the funeral home's doors.

Annie shook her head. "No. It's peaceful. It's just the sort of place a troubled spirit would go to overcome the trauma of her death."

Adam gave her a concerned look but said nothing.

Inside the funeral home, an elderly woman sat at the reception. She had lovely silver-blue hair and wore a cozy, hand-knit cardigan wrapped around her frail frame. Annie smiled at her as she stepped up to the desk.

"Hello," she greeted. "I'm Annie, and this is my friend, Detective Adam Parker. Could we have a few minutes of your time?"

The receptionist stared at her blankly while Adam cleared his throat.

"Who are you talking to?" Adam asked.

"The..." Annie trailed off as she inspected the receptionist. Her skin was almost luminous, and the silvery tones to her weren't because of old age at all. She blushed. "Oh, I am sorry."

Adam touched her wrist. "Annie?"

She turned to him, shaking her head. "There's a spirit here. I mistook her for a receptionist."

"I am, of sorts," the woman said as she stood. "Sorry, most people don't see me. Hold on, dear, I'll go get Robert."

"Thank you," Annie said hesitantly.

The ghost floated through the wall, and Annie turned to Adam. His expression was hard and suspicious. She hated seeing him look like that. "You believe me, don't you?"

"I... want to believe," Adam hedged.

Annie's stomach plummeted. He thought she was a liar. Did this mean that every time he called her *Little Witch*, it was teasing? She thought he believed in her magic, but was he pretending all this time?

She didn't have the chance to ask, as at that moment the ghost returned, through the door to the back this time. Seconds later, the door opened, and a middle-aged man with greying hair and bright, intelligent eyes entered.

"Hello," he greeted. He leaned on an elegant cane as he walked over and offered his hand to Adam. "I'm Robert Jenson. How may I help you?"

CHAPTER 5

Adam looked suspiciously over the mortician, though he fought to keep his expression smooth and emotionless. He trusted Annie too much to believe she was trying to pull the wool over his eyes, but everything was just so exhausting.

After he failed to save Isabella Turner, he didn't want to think about spirits wandering the world, lost. Adam wasn't exactly a religious guy, but he believed in heaven. His heart ached to think that a young woman who had already lost so much at the hands of Jonathan Swift would be lost from heaven simply because he hadn't arrived in time to save her.

Was it even possible to be barred from eternal rest? Shouldn't only those who have to make up for their past mistakes have the unrest of wandering about the Earth, unable to move on?

He shook his head slightly. Robert looked perfectly respectable. He had kind eyes and a resting smile that would put mourners at ease.

"Have you ever done business with a man named Jonathan Swift?" Adam asked.

"Jonathon?" Robert's brows furrowed. "Yes, actually. We handled his wife's funeral some six years ago. He comes in on the anniversary of her death every year to buy another casket."

Annie leaned forward, but her eyes were on the space beside Robert. "Don't you find that strange?"

Robert turned, and they both watched the blank space before Robert nodded. "That's right."

"What is?" Adam asked, fighting back the irritation.

Annie winced. "Sorry. I forgot to tell you. Adam can't see spirits."

Adam's gaze roved the empty room. "There's someone with us?"

"My mother, Gertrude," Robert offered.

"A spirit," Adam clarified.

Annie slid her hand into his and squeezed. He appreciated the physical comfort—his head was spinning. He squeezed back, giving her a small, thankful smile. But his heart was heavy. Had Isabella moved on? Or was she still trying to find her way?

"Yes. She only passed recently and wanted to make sure Robert got himself taken care of before moving on." She paused, then nodded. "Jonathon told them he was buying the caskets to give to other young families who unexpectedly lost a loved one. They didn't find it strange because it seemed like a sweet tradition."

Adam processed the information as he pulled a picture from his pocket and showed it to Robert. "Have you seen this woman? Her name is Yasmine Delisle?"

"Yasmine?" Robert's brow furrowed, and he shook his head. "I can't recall seeing her before. Mother?"

Adam glanced at Annie, who shook her head slightly.

It wasn't the news he wanted to hear. As far as his investigation had told him, Jonathon had lived with his wife just outside of the city. He moved around to find his victims, so he still had no proof that Jonathon had taken Yasmine… nor was he any closer to finding where she was buried.

"Did you notice anything strange out of the ordinary?" Annie urged, looking from the space to Robert. "Anything you might think of will be helpful to know."

Robert clucked his tongue. "Come to think of it, yes. He recently had an order for another casket, even though the anniversary of his wife's passing was already over."

Adam's heart gave a sudden, hard thump. "How many has he bought over the years?"

"Seven or eight, I should think," Robert said. He looked between Adam and Annie. "I'm sorry, but I'm baffled about what is happening here. Is Jonathon in some sort of trouble? And why did you say he *claimed* to be giving them to other families?"

Annie blew a heavy breath and looked at Adam, her eyes pleading. She was so bright and full of life; it was hard for her to express these things. Adam, unfortunately, had far more experience.

"Jonathan Swift was recently taken into custody for the murder of a young woman named Isabella Turner. I believe he has had at least five other victims. Knowing how many caskets he purchased from you may help us find the bodies of the other woman." He kept his expression neutral, his tone calm. People didn't respond well to any emotion in these sorts of circumstances.

Annie nodded once. "It's unfortunately true. I contacted Yasmine in my dreams last night, and she led me here. It's why I was hoping you'd have seen her.

Robert, looking distinctly shaken, headed for the computer at the reception. "Hold on; I can get you my records. I can't believe it. Jonathon seemed like such a nice young man... deeply mourning his wife but...."

He sat at the computer and rapidly typed on it.

"Thank you," Adam said.

Robert printed the sales records and handed them over to Adam. "Eight. He bought eight caskets from us, starting six years ago with his wife."

Adam's heart hammered even harder into his ribs. He barely thanked Robert again before he turned on his heel and strode away. Annie raced after him. Her expression was worried, her gaze never leaving his face.

"What is it?" she asked him.

"There's someone else."

Annie tossed him her keys and slid into the passenger side door. Adam had to adjust the position of the driver's seat before he got in after her. Annie had plugged a new address into the GPS by that time, and the electronic voice gave Adam directions.

"What do you mean, there's someone else?"

Adam's grip tightened on the wheel. "Eight caskets. One for his wife. Five for the missing women we've already connected to him. One for Isabella. That's only seven. We're missing someone. Someone he took before Isabella... or maybe after."

"But you arrested him on site, didn't you?" Annie asked, her eyes wide.

Adam's mind rushed in circles. "Isabella had been dead for about an hour when we found her. And Jonathon Swift was caught driving back into town. But with her injuries, Isabella could have been lying on that floor for days before she actually passed."

"Oh, Adam," Annie breathed. She twisted her hands together. "Yasmine didn't tell me anything about another person. But..."

Was there a chance? A seventh victim that could still be alive?

"Where are we going?" he asked his voice tense.

"To where he's keeping Yasmine." Annie shuddered visibly. "Adam...?"

Adam heard the question in her voice, but he had no room to answer. So he pressed harder on the gas, increasing their speed. Even though he knew chances were, they were already too late.

Annie kept feeling colder and colder as they grew nearer to their destination. When she recognized the buildings from her dream, her teeth began chattering. Pain throbbed through her stomach, and she bit back the urge to tell Adam to turn around, to take her away from here.

I have to do this, she reminded herself.

4738 was soon in view. Adam abruptly stopped in front of it and hurried around the car to open Annie's door. He helped her out, his expression concerned.

"Are you all right, Little Witch?'"

Annie made herself smile. "Yeah. Let's go in."

They headed up the driveway when suddenly, a figure melted

through the doorway. Yasmine stood there; her hands clenched into fists. "Hurry!" she called.

Annie broke into a run.

"The key is under the mat," Yasmine said, pointing.

Annie kicked aside the mat and grabbed the key. She shoved it into the lock and opened the door before Adam caught up. The pain was getting worse. She was so cold she expected to see ice coating her skin. As she stumbled in, Yasmine hovered behind her.

"In the basement, behind the blue door," Yasmine said urgently

"Basement," Annie gasped, falling to her knees. "Blue door. Go!"

"Annie—" Adam said urgently.

"Go!"

Adam rushed past her. Yasmine stood where she was, looking anxiously down the dark stairs. A rush of warmth suddenly washed over Annie's frame. She sighed in relief, lifting her face.

"Call the ambulance," Yasmine told Annie. "She'll need it."

Annie dialed 9-1-1 without question, even though she could hardly speak.

One by one, five other women appeared. Tears hit Annie's eyes as she recognized each of Jonathon's victims. Last of all was Isabella Turner, with her arms wrapped around herself, watching the basement as Adam came back up, carrying a limp form in his arms.

"What...?" Annie asked, but as she blinked, the women were gone.

"She's alive," Adam said as he laid the limp figure onto the carpeted floor. He yanked off his coat and spread it over her. "He had her locked in a freezer room with their caskets. But she's alive, Annie... alive!"

CHAPTER 6

Annie accompanied the young woman to the hospital, while Adam stayed at the house to apprise the Chicago police of what was happening. The woman was nearly frozen to death and badly malnourished and dehydrated, but the doctors said she would make it.

After a few hours, Adam met Annie at the hospital. Jonathan Swift's six victims had disappeared except one. Isabella sat beside the young woman, watching her while Annie dozed in a chair.

Isabella wore a full-length black coat; the same one she had been wearing when Jonathan Swift took her. Annie recognized it now. It had been the one she saw on the mysterious figure who had left the wake quickly without talking to anyone. Isabella had been there; Annie just hadn't realized it at the time.

"I talked to the doctors," Adam murmured as he handed Annie a cup of coffee. "We got to her just in time. I wish Isabella had been as lucky… I wish I had found her in time."

Isabella looked up. "He blames himself? He shouldn't. I was going to die, anyway. I wasn't quite all the way gone when he got there. And I could see his sorrow. I didn't die alone because of him, and I will be forever grateful for that."

Annie took Adam's hand. She wasn't sure how he was going to take it. "Isabella's here."

Adam stiffened.

"She wants you to know that she doesn't blame you. She's just happy that you could find her. Your presence was a comfort to her as she died."

Adam still didn't relax.

"Did you find out her identity?" Annie asked, hoping to distract him.

"No. We searched the premises and found the other women in the caskets, but there was no sign of who this young woman is." Adam passed a hand over his eyes. "I hope she wakes soon so we can reunite her with her family."

Isabella seemed to fade somewhat, then came back into complete focus next to Adam's shoulder. "I know who she is."

Annie's hand tightened on Adam's reflexively. "Isabella knows her."

Adam's brow furrowed. "How?"

"Her name is Elizabeth Martinelli, and she's my twin sister. We were adopted," Isabella added, looking back to the sleeping form on the bed. "She didn't have a good life as I did. I contacted her, and we were talking, cautiously learning about each other, before that man...."

"They were twin sisters, given up for adoption," Annie explained to Adam. "They hadn't ever met, but I guess Swift must have gotten access to their records. Since they were both born the day his wife died, he went for both of them. Isabella was more like his wife, though, so he focused on her. Why would he have bought another casket for Elizabeth, though?"

Adam shook his head. "I don't think he was looking for his wife. At the house, we found a bunch of books on necromancy; I think he was trying to bring her back to life."

"Oh." Annie shifted closer to the detective, another shudder running down her spine.

She now understood that her vision connected her to Elizabeth rather than Yasmine. It had all been so confusing, but that was why she had been so cold and in pain. Even though the potion hadn't worked exactly as she wanted, she was still happy with the results.

A woman was alive now because of them. And that was all that mattered.

Several days later, with further evidence of Jonathan Swift's crimes and Elizabeth's testimony, he pleaded guilty and was sentenced to a lifetime in prison with no parole. Annie was glad that such a dangerous man would never be on the streets again.

Isabella and the others moved on, or at least Annie thought they did. It made her wonder what was keeping Monty around. Maybe one day, she would ask him about it.

Today, though, she was already in his bad books. Adam was coming over for dinner, and Monty continually expressed his displeasure by knocking things off the counter.

"Why don't you go watch a movie?" Annie complained as she picked up a pile of letters for the fifth time.

Monty narrowed his eyes at her and folded his arms.

"Adam believes you're here now," she added, hoping that would make a difference.

No such luck. He knocked a glass of water over. Annie bit back a curse as she rushed to mop up the water. Monty glared a moment longer before he stalked off through the wall. Annie huffed a breath, wishing she knew what was wrong with him.

Adam showed up a little while later, bringing a bottle of wine and a salad to go with the meatloaf and potatoes Annie had prepared. She quickly set the table, and Adam poured the wine as they sat up to eat.

"Do you want to talk about the Swift, or are you done for the day?" Annie asked him.

"We can talk about it. All the women he killed were identified and have been returned to their families for burial." Adam set the wine bottle down and smiled at her. He looked as though a great weight had been lifted off his shoulders. "And you? Any other visions?"

Annie shook her head. "It seemed like when I replaced all my spices and herbs; it got rid of whatever was tainting them to give me spontaneous visions. I'll keep working on the potion I used to find Elizabeth, though. It will be good to control these things."

Adam cut his meatloaf into bite-sized pieces. "But is it safe? We've never really talked about magic. At first, I thought you were playing, but this case has forced me to look at this. It's all real, isn't it?"

"Yes." Annie lowered her fork. "Did you think I was lying?"

"I tried not to think of it at all, if I'm honest."

"I see."

Adam must have heard the disappointment in her voice because he looked up quickly. "I never believed in any of this stuff, not even when I was a kid. I was a facts man. But you turn me upside down in more ways than one, Annie. Sometimes, I don't know what to do."

Surprise rippled through her. It was the last confession that she had expected tonight. Butterflies erupted in her stomach. "I... don't always know what to do around you, either. I thought you would dismiss me when I said I was a witch. But you trust me. That... means a lot."

Her fingers crept across the table toward him.

"Well... I'm still waiting," he said gruffly, his usually calm demeanor broken by the blush on his cheeks. "Are these potions safe?"

"Yes," Annie said promptly.

And they were... mostly. Annie still had the occasional icy chill creep over her, but it never lasted long. Besides, there were bound to be some side effects of the potions. At least this way, she could monitor herself.

"I'd feel better if your mentor... Rosemary, was it?"

"Yeah."

"If she could come and give you a magical checkup, I don't know." Adam frowned as he chewed his meatloaf. "Do they have magical checkups?"

Annie laughed and waved a hand. "You're worrying too much, Adam. I'm perfectly fine. I know what I'm doing. Potions don't change a person; they open up the body's natural systems to be receptive to what is normally shut out."

Adam leaned forward. "Does that mean you could make a potion to make me have your visions instead?"

Annie drew back in shock. Was he being serious, or was this a test?

Was he seeing if it was safe, as she claimed? The truth was that she wouldn't give Adam a potion that hadn't been rigorously tested.

Concern twisted her stomach. Was she playing with forces beyond her power? She had been using her magic to help Adam solve his cases before she started having visions. Was it such a bad idea to take the potion to Rosemary and put it through some peer review? Was she taking unnecessary risks herself?

Prophecy can't be created. If it's invoking these visions, it just means it's opening up my mind enough to tap into an ability I already have. I need the potions to help me get to where I can tap into my visions without them.

She laughed as she playfully shoved Adam's shoulder. "Oh, I see what you're doing!"

"What?"

Annie gave him an impish grin as she sipped her wine. "You're hoping you can use my potions to give yourself visions and cut me out of the fun part."

"Hey," Adam protested. "That's not—"

"You want all the glory to yourself," Annie continued teasingly, "Detective Adam Parker, the new Sherlock Holmes. Cut out the middleman and receive the visions straight to your head."

Adam rolled his eyes. "Oh, I see how it is. You want me to keep begging you for help."

His tone took on a teasing lilt and Annie ignored the lingering worry in his eyes. She stood up and spread her arms as though addressing a massive crowd. "Ladies and gentlemen, I present you the dynamic detective duo. Annie and Adam! We'll solve your murder!"

Adam clapped. "Brava, brava!"

Annie bowed to him, happy that the conversation had turned. She retook her seat and tasted the salad. The dressing was creamy and sweet, with just a hint of sourness at the aftertaste. She grinned.

"This is delicious," she told Adam.

"Thanks. It's my grandmother's recipe."

Annie latched onto the topic. "How is she doing?"

"Up to her usual hijinks," Adam chuckled.

They fell into the familiar pattern of discussing family and plans for the next few days. Adam would be building that raised garden bed he promised on the weekend, and Annie was already plotting how she would plant the herbs from her garden.

At one point, Monty ducked into the dining room again. Annie pointed him out, and Adam greeted him politely, but Monty only left again without communicating. Annie made up some lies to make her roommate not seem rude, and the rest of the evening passed in laughter and fun.

Well, after dark, Adam decided it was time to go home. Annie walked him to the door, and he stood half in and half out. A beautiful full moon hung in the sky outside.

"I always loved the full moon," Adam whispered. He turned back to her and smiled at her. "Goodnight, Little Witch."

His hand came up, and he brushed his thumb over her cheekbone. Sparks tingled under her skin, and warmth blossomed from the place he touched her. Adam's eyes were in darkness, so that she couldn't see him. His fingers slid down her cheek, tucking under her chin. He lifted her face to his. For a moment, she thought he was going to lean forward.

But then his hand dropped, and he walked down the front path to his car. Her heart slammed into her chest, feeling off balance as Adam drove away. She touched her cheek where his warmth lingered, then turned back into her house.

A smile blossomed over her face. She locked the door and went to clean up the dining room. Another case successfully closed, a woman's life was saved, and a new potion she could use to save others. And best of all, a fantastic night with Adam Parker.

How could life get any better than this?

The End

MURDERED ON HALLOWEEN

A JANE AND KENNEDY DANIELS MYSTERY

CHAPTER 1

For most, October 31st, aka Halloween, marks the start of the holiday season. It starts the countdown to Christmas and New Year's. Jane Daniels had always been a bit of a sleuth. She loved mysteries, crime novels, and drama. One of her favourite pastimes was curling up on the sofa with her wife, Kennedy, to watch serial killer documentaries while piecing everything together before the celebrity narrator revealed the killer. The fact that Kennedy enjoyed the same was one of the things that had first attracted Jane to her wife. Jane and Kennedy met in college while Kennedy was on an exchange program. It was love at first sight. They both loved mysteries, and Jane had a talent for solving crimes. Jane looked at mysteries as puzzles, seeing them as just missing that vital piece. And she needed to find it.

But she also loved a good bargain. She loved hunting around shops for that bargain item she could brag about. She considered every shopping expedition an excuse to hunt for treasure. The X on her mental treasure map always turned out to be the location of the most discounted item in the particular store she was in. Jane loved hunting thrift shops around Halloween. She would find missed and forgotten outfits and pieces that she could craft into the perfect Halloween costume. A piece that was one of a kind. And this year was no exception. The mayor had invited Jane and Kennedy to the big Halloween celebration. Jane was determined that this year's costumes would be better than ever.

Meanwhile, Kennedy was the cyber-wizard of the family. She loved it when Jane came home with a new gadget. She loved nothing more than to add something new to her electronics collection, especially something that she could use to make everyday life easier and more enjoyable. Kennedy had practically automated every inch of their home. It was like living in the future. Having a top-notch home meant they had more time to spend with each other, which helped them stay close as a couple.

Kennedy's favourite part of Halloween was creating a new, scary contraption to spook the trick or treaters with. At first, Jane thought it was cruel until she saw how much the children looked forward to seeing what would jump out at them this year.

Kennedy was a reasonably intelligent woman. She was very proud of her M.I.T. education. Her keen intellect was why Detective Inspector Arthur Gottfried often consulted her regarding some of his more complex crime cases. She had helped on several occasions that year alone, and even more since she had moved to the U.K. full time from her home in Boston, Massachusetts.

Jane and Kennedy had a lot in common, making their marriage strong, but they had other interests, which kept them from butting heads. Jane *loved* to bake. Something about baking was so relaxing and calming. And although Kennedy was a bit of an introvert, she managed to find her passion too. Coding gave her a sense of control and allowed her to explore the most that her mind had to offer. Their friends always admired the love they had for each other. As a result, their friends often referred to their successful marriage as *#couplegoals*.

For her part, Jane was a little jealous of the families that their friends were raising, wanting one of her own, but she never let it show. She was happy being 'fun aunty Jane' for the time being. Holidays and special occasions were her favourite time of year, and with Halloween fast approaching, her excitement grew.

She loved having all the children dressed up, knocking on her door and singing, "Trick or Treat!" Even Kennedy got involved with decorating the house. Kennedy took great pleasure in making the house as scary as possible, trying to outdo herself every year. For Jane, it was the chorus of laughter when the kids realised it was fake and the shrieks of glee when they were given fistfuls of candy that she loved most.

Jane would love nothing more than to have a child before her biological clock started to slow down. Lately, this had begun to be more of a pressing issue for Jane. Though on the surface, she'd accepted that this was not quite the right time for the Daniels family to have children. She buried herself in sleuthing and finding new gadgets to help them in their daily life and around the home, pretending that the ache to have a child would go away if she kept busy enough.

"OK, hon, here it is. The costumes to beat all costumes," Jane cheered, placing Kennedy's costume on the big armchair in the corner of the room.

Kennedy walked over and unpacked the costume with an eye roll and loving smirk. Brown pants with a tail attached, a matching jacket that, once fastened, completed a torso and a headpiece that could be worn covering the face or not. It didn't take much for Kennedy to piece the costume together. The large teal collar with the gold-plated tag gave the identity away. It was a Scooby-Doo costume!

"I know you said something simple, and you wanted a mask, but when I saw this, I thought it would be super cute. And if the trick or treaters knocked before we left for the party, they would love it too," Jane cheered, pulling her costume out of the bag and twirling around the room in "I used to love watching Scooby and the gang when I was little," she reminisced.

"I said I didn't want to be recognised. This is a full-blown disguise! I don't think my mother would recognise me in this," Kennedy exclaimed.

"Exactly, it's a costume ball. How often do we get invited to such things? We have to make the most of it," Jane chimed, trying on her matching mask over her eyes.

"I'll give you this. I love seeing how excited you get about these things," Kennedy smiled.

Kennedy wasn't much of a party person. She much preferred her wife's company and her few close friends. Hence, she wanted a mask; less chance of people stopping to talk if they didn't know who she was. But Kennedy often went to parties she didn't want to, purely to make Jane happy. Seeing Jane happy and excited always made the parties worthwhile. Even Kennedy had to admit that the mayor's ball was a once-in-a-lifetime event this year. So, she would be a fool to miss out.

"So, which member of the Scooby gang will you be?" Kennedy asked, sitting on the footstool, watching Jane play about with her ensemble and examining her outfit in more detail, still not fully understanding it. Her eyebrows were slightly furrowed, and the teal from the collar reflected off her blue eyes.

"Well, I thought couple's costumes would be fun. But I don't know if I can pull off Shaggy. So, I picked up a Shaggy costume and a Daphne costume. What do you think?" Jane smiled.

Kennedy grinned, "While I love the idea of us going as Shaggy and Scooby, I do love you in purple." Jane didn't look much like Daphne, she had brown hair and wasn't quite as thin, but she would have pulled it off well.

"I love me in purple too. But if we are doing couples costumes and we already have Shaggy and Scooby, one of us will *have* to be Shaggy. How fun will it be to be completely unrecognisable for a night? It will be fun," Jane nodded enthusiastically.

"Flip for it? Heads Shaggy, tails Scooby?" Kennedy laughed, pulling a pound coin from her jeans pocket, hiding the laugh at Jane's expression. She put the coin back before flipping it. Kennedy knew that Jane wouldn't want to be Scooby. Even if she dressed as Shaggy, Jane would still find a way to add a touch of feminine glamour to the outfit. Kennedy burst out laughing.

"Don't worry, sweetie, you can be Shaggy," Kennedy smiled.

"You're not mad?" Jane asked.

"What would I be mad at? I think all of this is hilarious," Kennedy laughed.

"Why?"

"Here I thought we were going to a Halloween party dressed as ghosts with sheets over our heads. You know, simple."

Jane burst out laughing at Kennedy's crazy suggestion.

"Plus, even in a mask and being unrecognisable, I am still going with the prettiest woman in the room," Kennedy winked. She loved flirting with her wife. Even after all this time, Jane still blushed like a schoolgirl.

Kennedy was tall and slender with deep black skin and beautiful ringlets that rested just above her elbows. Jane wasn't exaggerating; her wife was a total catch, and she knew it.

This was no ordinary Halloween party. It was an exclusive Halloween ball hosted by the mayor. The town's most significant, brightest, and elite would be there. It was a chance to meet some new people, some influential people. Sheets with eye holes would not cut it. While the primary goal of the evening was to have fun and relax, Kennedy was looking forward to making some new connections and treating the party as a networking event, much to Jane's annoyance.

The party in question was to be held at one of the most famous hotels in London – The Mandarin.

The Mandarin was known for being the place for celebrities and world royals. It was a hotel steeped in history, extravagance, and luxury. Every day, it was crowded with fans hoping to catch a glimpse of their favourite pop star or movie star, sporting heroes, or just to glimpse how the other half lived.

The mayor herself was hosting, Mayor Clara Porter. It was to be a night to relax and have fun. The mayor had only invited the most influential people in the city to join in the night's festivities. Kennedy and Jane thought it was odd that the party was so exclusive but theorised that the mayor created an opportunity to meet her favourite celebrities and didn't want other folks to get in her way.

Rumour had it that there was to be a live band, someone pretty famous, performing for the night. The guest list had been kept strictly confidential. It was the talk of London who would be going to such a party.

Jane had assumed that the only reason she and Kennedy had been invited was because of Kennedy's ongoing help with Detective Arthur Gottfried. Kennedy worked as a freelance programmer, and occasionally Detective Gottfried needed help with working on new technology for his office or, more likely, to gather information about their latest suspect. Throughout their working relationship, the girls and Arthur had bonded and considered themselves close friends.

No matter the reason for the invite, Jane was excited to go. Kennedy's invitation was ambiguous and didn't directly state whether Jane was invited to the event, but Jane was sure Kennedy would get crafty if they ran into any problems. The invitation said the theme of the party was "Halloween Horrors." It was exciting to think about the decorations that would be inside. Even though Kennedy usually made Halloween decorations, seeing some at the event would still be fun.

However, she did feel slightly disappointed at missing out on the trick-or-treating fun with the neighbourhood kids this year. When the kids found out that there would be no haunted house decorating the front yard and no spooky traps jumping out at them, they were disappointed. But when Jane promised that she would get autographs if any of their favourite celebrities attended, the kids soon perked up again.

Every reporter, social media influencer, and gossip rag had followed Mayor Porter around for the last two months while she organised the event, hunting like vultures for any minute detail they could publish. Eventually, Mayor Porter decided to give them a little taste of the evening.

"The bar shall only be servicing beer and wine and will close at 11 p.m. I don't want anyone driving home drunk. Taxis will be supplied for everyone and anyone over the limit. That will be all," Mayor Porter announced.

The small gathering of reporters grunted with disappointment.

They had hoped for something juicy to get the readers flipping the pages or subscribers watching videos. But Mayor Porter was known for keeping her cards close to her chest. So, all that anyone outside of a strict handful of people knew was the location, the date, that it was a costume ball, and now that the bar would close at eleven.

"Come on, Mayor Porter! Just one name! An industry even. Will there be athletes there? Movie stars?" begged the paparazzi.

"I can neither confirm nor deny," Mayor Porter grinned, taking great pleasure in making the media squirm.

CHAPTER 2

The taxi pulled up outside The Mandarin, leaving Jane and Kennedy to gasp and awe at the decorations. Police lined the streets holding back fans hoping to spot celebrities and paparazzi hoping to catch a snap of the guests. A long red carpet lined the pavement from the drop-off point to the large golden double doors. Performers dressed as ghouls danced with fire while others showed off their fire-breathing skills, keeping everyone outside entertained. Lights leapt across the sky above the hotel. Goosebumps pricked Jane and Kennedy's skin. They knew that tonight would be a night they would never forget.

Stepping out of the taxi, the pair were relieved to have opted for costumes involving masks. It gave them a sense of privacy that they imagined the celebrity guests didn't get too often. Blinding flashes of lights erupted around them as the paparazzi made every effort to capture their picture.

"I kind of feel like a celebrity myself," Jane grinned.

"Let's give them a show, shall we? Enjoy our fifteen seconds of fame?" Kennedy chuckled.

"Look! Over there! Who are you?" yelled one paparazzi as he flashed his camera.

"Take off the mask!" yelled another.

They gave the crowd a quick wave, striking a few poses and hearing them scream their approval. Blinking back the blinding lights of hundreds of cameras, Jane and Kennedy chuckled as they headed to the door.

A tall, distinguished gentleman in a royal blue suit, hat, and white gloves with a gold chain attached to his pocket watch smiled at them as they approached. Kennedy was surprised that the doorman wasn't in fancy dress, considering everyone else in and around the building was. Even the security team wore Halloween costumes, which Jane found very amusing. She imagined the big beefy security guard, who was dressed as a clown, chasing someone down the street, stifling a laugh as the thought took over her mind.

"Good evening, do you have an invitation?" he asked with a slight bow of his head.

"Yes, here you go," Jane smiled, pulling the invitation from her purse.

One quick look over, he nodded and opened the door.

"Head left at the sign and follow the arrows to the grand ballroom. Enjoy your evening, Mrs and Mrs Daniels."

"Thank you," Kennedy smiled back, offering her hand to shake.

The doorman winked and smiled back, quietly placing the tip that Kennedy had slid him into his pants pocket. She had seen the move done several times in movies, but her favourite was in her guilty pleasure – F.R.I.E.N.D.S. reruns. She had been waiting so long for an opportunity to try it. It was fun to get a taste of how the rich and famous live.

When Jane and Kennedy reached the ballroom, they were amazed that it spanned two floors. A large spiral staircase separated the two, with black, purple, and orange decorations. A large chandelier hung from the ceiling, and a small gathering of guests dressed in an array of ornate costumes donned the dance floor below. A band was set up and playing from the main stage; they were all dressed in costume. Jane had been looking forward to seeing who the mystery band performing would be, but their costumes concealed their identities. Jane looked forward to figuring out who the singers were all evening.

Jane and Kennedy stood at the top of the staircase, admiring the room. The door closing behind them alerted the other guests to their arrival; all eyes in the room drifted up to them, watching with beaming smiles as they descended the staircase of the far wall of the dance floor.

The room was like nothing either of them had seen before. Surrounding the dance floor sat rows of tables filled with couples who were not ready to start dancing yet. As they drew further down the stairs, the decorations came into view. The mayor had worked her magic. The room was decorated like a haunted house. Pedestals scattered the room with performers dressed as ghouls and ghosts., jumping out at guests who got too close. Each performer twirled ribbons, buttons, or hoops, giving the guests a show like no other. Small glass cages scattered across the bar area filled with snakes and spiders. Kennedy hoped they were fake as she wasn't too fond of snakes, nor Jane of spiders. It wasn't until later that evening that they found out the local zoo had loaned the creatures out for the evening.

"This is incredible," Jane whispered to Kennedy.

"It's like entering another world," Jane awed.

"I know, Mayor Porter has impressed me," Kennedy admitted.

Kennedy may have been reluctant to go to the party at first. But now that she was there, she found she was looking forward to the rest of the evening and was glad that Jane had insisted on them going. Kennedy admired the animatronics that flew around the room as the tech geek she was. Small drones were operating mechanical witches, ghouls, and ghosts. There really was something for everyone there that evening.

As soon as they reached the bottom step, they were immediately greeted by a stranger dressed as Fred from the Scooby gang. Whoever he was appeared to have been waiting for them, tucked in the shadows of the stairs. He jumped out with such enthusiasm that both Kennedy and Jane jumped, startled before chuckling to themselves.

"You guys look amazing," he laughed heartily.

"Arthur, you look incredible. All we need now is a Daphne and Velma. We have the entire Scooby gang," Jane laughed, admiring how well Arthur pulled off the ascot and blonde wig.

"Great minds shop alike," Arthur beamed, showing off his costume. He was obviously very proud of his effort. "Scooby and Shaggy, a great combination. You both look fantastic."

Jane giggled back happily while Kennedy offered a proud bow. But, of course, Arthur would see right through their disguises. He was a phenomenal detective, after all.

"This venue is incredible; it must be costing the city a mint to host such an extravagant ball," Kennedy said, stepping aside as more guests descended the stairs.

"Nah, everyone has chipped in. The fire department, the police, and other emergency services. We helped decorate and even paid for some of the snacks and cocktails. It's nothing fancy, but we felt we should do our part," Arthur replied.

Jane and Kennedy nodded back, their eyes dancing around the room, admiring the show.

"Madame Mayor has done us proud. We are all here to have fun. So come on, let's have some fun," Arthur laughed, heading off into the crowd.

It wasn't long before Jane and Kennedy lost Arthur in the crowd, but they had no doubt they would see him again as the night drew on.

An hour later, the party was in full swing. The dance floor was full of dancing couples. A small selection of paparazzi had been let inside, closely monitored by the Mayor's P.R. team.

Many of the officers had invited friends to join the fun. Everyone had made an extra effort to disguise themselves—guests dressed as pirates, ghosts, vampires, and zombies.

The room was a mix of characters. While the Daniels' admired the

Halloween-themed costumes, Jane loved the extravagance of some of the more elaborate and glamorous outfits. There was a Cleopatra donned in heaps of gold and turquoise jewellery. A Mary Queen of Scots, a Joan of Arc, Greek goddesses, and movie stars. Even Mayor Clara Porter looked stunning, dressed as Marie Antoinette.

The selection was truly unique. There was even another Scooby-Doo in the same costume. The only difference between Kennedy and the other Scooby-Doo was the shoes. Kennedy wore red Sabot-like shoes, pointed at the toe with a red leather-pressed bow and gold short metal studs, with a small heel so she could feel a little feminine in the dog costume. The gentleman who wore the same outfit had opted for emerald-green velvet slippers.

I wish I had opted for slippers, Kennedy pondered.

Kennedy rarely wore high heels. While she was steady on her feet, she much preferred an excellent pair of comfortable flat shoes. Despite the short kitten-like heel on her shoes, her feet ached as she danced the night away with her wife.

CHAPTER 3

Two hours later, the evening was still going strong. Everyone was having the night of fun, relaxation, and networking that the mayor had planned. The night was proving to be a huge success. The band played *I Put a Spell on You*, *The Monster Mash*, and other Halloween-themed songs between more upbeat tunes, giving the guests a night to remember. Jane thought it was even more fun when songs like *Thriller* were played, and everyone joined in dancing in unison.

Jane and Kennedy danced the night away, and Kennedy made some new friends in the tech industry. Jane played off that she was annoyed Kennedy had brought her business cards. Secretly, she was proud that she had taken the initiative.

"I know I wasn't overly excited about tonight, but I'm happy you made me come," Kennedy smiled, kissing Jane softly on the forehead.

"See, I told you it would be fun. I'm just nipping to the ladies' room. Meet you at the bar when I get back?"

"Sure. Strawberry wine?" Kennedy replied.

Jane nodded back as she headed across the floor.

Jane headed to the ladies' room to freshen up her makeup and fix her hair. She smiled at her reflection and gave her wig a slight fluff up, and reapplied her makeup, beard, and eyeliner. She was preparing to head back to the party when she heard a woman's distressed scream coming from outside. Jane's heart pounded, her gut telling her something was amiss. The screams were not just those of a guest frightened by the night's festivities. Her inner voice told her to stay in the bathroom. But her heart ruled her head, and she followed the screams.

On the floor outside the men's bathroom, Jane saw a sight that stopped her heart cold. Panic, pain, and heartbreak ran through her as she looked at the Scooby-Doo lying on the floor with a bloodied hole staining the teal dog collar. A woman dressed as Velma cradled the body, covered in blood. The mask was untouched and perfect. The painted eyes looked even more haunting now that the life behind them was gone.

Tears streamed from Jane's eyes as she launched herself at the body on the floor, clawing at the jacket collar.

"Kennedy? Kennedy, what happened?" Jane cried.

"Kennedy? Why do you keep calling my husband that?" the woman cradling the body and shot her an icy look, her voice laced with pain and anger as confusion filled her eyes.

Jane stood, staring down at the body. Scanning, she noticed the green velvet slippers. The body wasn't Kennedy. Jane was suddenly racked with guilt. She felt relieved that the body lying dead on the floor wasn't her wife. She felt awful for feeling that way, even though she knew it was a normal human reaction. Her heart went out to the woman rocking back and forth, holding her husband.

"I'm so sorry…. you are right; that's not my wife. I'm so very, very sorry," Jane sobbed.

She scanned the crowd that flocked towards the commotion, hoping to see Kennedy and ease her pounding heart.

A small crowd of guests had gathered around the body, everyone curious about what had happened. Most thought it was all part of the evening—a show or a murder mystery, in fact. Shock quickly spread when realisation sunk in, and everyone was forced to admit someone had been murdered at the party. All too shocked and concerned to pull themselves away from the horror.

"Hold it, folks," boomed Arthur Gottfried's voice.

He pushed through the crowd, pulling off his ascot and wig and discarding them on a nearby table, instantly shifting from party mode to detective mode.

"This is now an active crime scene. Many of you know what that means," Arthur said, pushing the crowd back as several other officers rushed forward, surrounding the scene with yellow crime scene tape.

"Only the M.E. and assigned officers are allowed past the yellow tape. So now everyone, please step back," Detective Gottfried boomed.

The guests knew what that meant. Many of them would be questioned and asked to go to the precinct to give a statement. Everyone at the party was now a suspect. The ballroom was locked down. No one was allowed to leave, and no one was allowed to enter until the scene had been examined.

Meanwhile, Madame Mayor was none too pleased, "Who is this man?" she asked Detective Gottfried.

"My husband, Judge Rainford," sniffled the dead man's wife.

"My condolences, Mrs Rainford. Please, follow me. Let's get you away from the crowd. Arthur, can I take her up to my suite?" the mayor asked.

"I will assign officers to accompany you," Arthur nodded.

Even the mayor was a suspect until proven otherwise. Arthur was reluctant to let her or the wife leave, assigning several officers to guard the mayor's suite, ensuring that they didn't make a run for it or become the next target.

As the judge's identity flew around the room on the crowd's whispers, speculation floated closely behind. Everyone assumed that the judge had been targeted because of his unflinching attitude towards prosecuting criminals and gang members. He had judged many high-profile cases that year alone, never mind the rest of his twenty-year career.

Everyone sat, frustrated, scared, and agitated—a wonderful night ending in horror. The theme of the night, Halloween horrors, had come to pass. Fitting yet, ironic.

As rumours circled the room, Jane's mind began to wander, and fear gripped her heart. Her mind raced back to the recent incident with Kennedy's car. The brakes had failed, and after inspection, they found they had been tampered with.

What if Kennedy was the intended target? What would have happened if the judge had not been wearing the same costume? Could the two events be related? Jane panicked.

Kennedy hadn't seemed to make the connection; she had removed her headpiece and mask and undone her jacket and collar, giving herself a little more space to breathe, given the tense situation.

"That costume was way hotter than I thought it would be," Kennedy complained, fanning herself with a drink menu from one of the tables.

Seeing Kennedy so calm settled Jane's mind a little; perhaps she was overthinking things, but she still couldn't help but worry, and she didn't want to worry Kennedy until she had more evidence.

The police gathered statements and CCTV footage from the hotel, staff, and guests. Then, as more and more suspects were cleared of any suspicion, the police began allowing people to leave. To most, the cause of death seemed obvious. But the medical examiner was confused about where the shot had come from. A bullet to the neck seemed straightforward, but not to Dr Albertson, who had been with the twelfth precinct for some eleven years.

"You see, Lieutenant," Dr Albertson began. "If the victim had been shot at close range, there would be burn marks around the wound even with a silencer. But instead, the bullet went right through, and it's a particular bullet from the recovered shell."

Lieutenant Gilbert Evans stood waiting, listening intently to what the M.E. had to say.

"It's not your typical handheld calibre. It looks more like it came from a rifle. I will know more for sure once I get the results back from the lab. This does, however, mean that the shooter was at a distance and above the victim. I believe the forensic teams need to investigate the Juliette balcony and the Mezzanine landing above the stairs. Hopefully, the shooter left some evidence behind."

If the shooter was on the stair landing or the Juliette balcony, how had nobody seen them? An amateur would be caught in no time. And an amateur couldn't have made a shot so accurate from so far away.

"Thank you, doctor; I will get the team right on it. It's going to be a long night," Evans sighed, his mind racing.

Is this shooter a professional? Arthur shook his head, pulled out a notepad, and began to scribble down his thoughts.

CHAPTER 4

The night had been long and tiresome. Detective Gottfried and Lieutenant Evans had left the party and headed straight to the precinct to begin their investigation. Lieutenant Evans had his suspicions, believing the bullet was a .22 calibre, but until he had spoken to the forensic team and had the report from the M.E., nothing was certain. He began to build a list of suspects: people from the party and people related to some of the judges' open cases. He was trying to create a map of connections, hoping he could find the common denominator to lead him to the shooter. The corkboard on his wall had photos of the party's attendees pinned to it, with strings connecting each photo to another.

"The C.S.I. teams are examining the upper floor this morning; I will let you know what they find as soon as I speak with them. Thank you, doctor. In the meantime, if you could give me the confirmation on the calibre of the bullet as soon as you can, I would appreciate it," Evans said, standing from the table in the medical examiner's office.

"I will send you my report as soon as I have it – Thanks for the coffee. It's exactly what I need after a sleepless night," Albertson yawned, leaving the room.

Later that afternoon, Evans was sitting in his office reviewing all the evidence that had been gathered. In such a short amount of time, it was impressive. Either his teams worked super hard, or the killer was sloppy. He smiled over the report; he had indeed been correct. The calibre of the bullet was a .22. This would prove to be a vital piece of evidence. The U.K. didn't have many guns, and even the forces were limited in their supply. Very few people had the expertise to control a weapon of such a calibre.

"This will make the list of suspects even smaller. We'll have this guy in no time," Evans smiled.

Evans often talked to himself in his office. He felt it helped him think clearer.

Meanwhile, back at the Daniels household, Jane had not been able to shake her feelings from the night before. She tried to tell herself that she was still in shock after the evening's events, which were now circulating on every news outlet and social media page. It felt suffocating. She wanted so badly to forget the judge's image dead on the floor. She tried to forget, even more, the pain in her chest when she thought it was Kennedy. Even thinking about it brought her back to tears. It seemed there would be no escape from the Halloween Horrors Ball.

With each news report, with details misinterpreted, Jane had more things to worry about. She still hadn't voiced her concerns to Kennedy. Pacing the kitchen, she did what she usually did when her mind spiralled. Pulling baking trays, cookie cutters, utensils, and mixing bowls from the kitchen cabinets, she began to remove ingredients from the fridge.

Baking always seemed to relax her. Her mind was so concentrated on measuring ingredients that there was no space left to worry. Without realising how much noise she was making, the slamming of tins on the counters brought Kennedy into the room.

She wrapped her arms around Jane's waist and kissed her wife softly on the cheek. She knew all too well that something was wrong when Jane became this chaotic.

"OK, sweetie, what's going on in that little head of yours? Are you hinting at new cake tins for Christmas?" Kennedy joked.

Jane spun around, looking lovingly up into Kennedy's eyes, her heart breaking at the thought that her concerns might have grounds.

"I think someone is trying to kill you," Jane choked.

Kennedy shrugged off the comment to Jane's horror, letting Jane go, and headed to the fridge to collect a fizzy drink. Little did Jane know, a similar thought had already crossed Kennedy's mind. But what sense would it make to worry her more?

"Don't do that, Jane. I know what you're thinking, and conjecture of this kind often leads to nothing. The judge and I wore the same costume – granted, but that means nothing. So why would I be a target?" Kennedy said, trying to soothe her wife.

Kennedy headed back to her home office. She wanted to get back to the new tech venture she was working on, thanks to the connections she made last night before all hell had broken loose.

"What about the brakes? They had been tampered with. Do you think that is a coincidence?" Jane insisted, following Kennedy inside, maintaining her stance.

With her querying gaze, Jane wanted Kennedy not to dismiss her concerns so lightly.

"Maybe, maybe not," Kennedy shrugged again.

"How can you dismiss this so easily?" Jane asked, alarmed.

"Look, when I took the car for its M.O.T., I picked it up from the garage after leaving a note for Charlie to send me the bill. The brakes were already marked as a concern, and Charlie had suggested I get them looked at as soon as possible. I planned to book them in after meeting with the guys from the tech convention a few days later. I simply forgot," Kennedy tried to reassure Jane, but nothing she said eased Jane's mind. "Purely coincidental."

Jane noted how Kennedy refused to meet her eye; Kennedy's gaze was planted on the floor. Jane knew that while Kennedy believed everything she said, she was still a little worried.

"I appreciate your concern, and I love you. I'm sure no one is after me. Whoever shot the judge will be apprehended soon enough. That will allay all your silly fears," Kennedy turned away, sitting at her desk and typing away, indicating the discussion was over.

Jane watched Kennedy for a few minutes before scoffing in frustration and noisily heading back to the kitchen to bake as loudly as possible.

Jane's concerns were not as ungrounded as Kennedy would have liked. Four days later, the police were no closer to apprehending the suspect. They had almost run out of leads and were drawing close to labelling it as a cold case.

Kennedy had headed out to a meeting with MedTech, a new medical technology company working on advanced medical equipment to aid in the recovery of injured soldiers in the field. The meeting was scheduled for two-thirty that afternoon in Kent. Kennedy was trying to be brave for Jane's sake, but after her outburst days before, Kennedy had made excuses not to use the car. So instead, Kennedy headed to the London Underground to catch her train.

Subconsciously, Kennedy walked through the streets of London with one eye constantly looking over her shoulder. Not watching where she was going, she almost walked into a mother and her baby coming up from the Underground.

"I'm so sorry, I wasn't watching where I was going," she apologised.

"It's OK. No one was hurt," smiled back the mother.

I'm paranoid, letting Jane's groundless concerns cloud my judgement, Kennedy thought, heading down past the turnstiles on the platform.

Her train was delayed. Pacing the platform to keep herself warm, Kennedy stopped, her heart pounding. A man stood in an alcove in a dark hooded leather jacket concealing most of his face. Usually, Kennedy would think nothing of it, but she had seen that figure before, following her from close to home. She had even seen him when she almost bumped into the mother just moments before.

Is he following me? Kennedy asked herself, trying to convince herself she was being paranoid.

Changing her path, moving between the crowd, she kept a close eye. Sure enough, the man followed. When Kennedy boarded her train, she lost sight of him. Looking through the train window, she was convinced she saw him still on the platform. Taking a breath, she sighed in frustration. *Purely paranoia.*

Listening to her music and scanning her notes for the rest of the journey, Kennedy allowed herself to relax, and excitement grew for her meeting. MedTech was using artificial intelligence and data science to reduce the number of misdiagnosed patients all around the globe. It was brilliant and would save the healthcare industry millions of pounds each year. Most importantly, it could help improve the quality of care for an unlimited number of patients. They were pushing for those funds to be rerouted into nurses' salaries.

She began to zone out, thinking about how incredible technology was. Closing her eyes, she leaned back and thought about how much life would improve over the next few decades. With A.I., the possibilities seemed endless.

Kennedy opened her eyes and was face to face with another mother and her twin babies. Her heart swelled, and she smiled. She realised that she wanted to have a baby, too. Kennedy had considered it before, of course, but hadn't seriously considered it until today. She shook her head and decided that she would talk to Jane after things had calmed down for them.

Her stop was nearing, and she was cutting it close to arriving at her meeting on time. She thought she had left early enough.

The figure she had seen at the first station reappeared as she packed her belongings into her bag and prepared to dismount at the next station.

Instinct kicked in, and she ducked out of the way. The blade missed her chest but sliced through her arm. Pain shot through her, and she cried out as blood began to pour down, soaking the floor as her heart beat faster in fear.

The train doors opened, and the figure took off. Kennedy ran down the platform after him, adrenaline pumping, holding tight to the gash in her arm, trying her best to control the bleeding. But unfortunately, the figure was too far ahead. He ran with the performance of a track runner, launching himself up the stairs, taking them two at a time.

"Hey, stop!" yelled a policeman who had followed Kennedy off the train, his partner charging passed, catching up on the figure as the two disappeared from sight.

"My partner has it covered. Let's get you to sit down and look at that wound," the policeman said, taking hold of Kennedy and leading her to a bench by the wall.

Sitting down, Kennedy took several slow, deep breaths to calm the adrenaline that flowed through her, making her tremble. *What was going on*? *What was happening*? Kennedy was confused, frustrated, and angry all at once.

"Now, why don't you tell me your name and what happened?" asked the policeman after he called on his radio for assistance.

CHAPTER 5

I t took roughly half an hour for the ambulance to get across the busy London streets in the afternoon. With rush hour traffic, Kennedy was honestly surprised it hadn't taken longer. Kennedy sat in the ambulance, contemplating what had happened after the E.M.T. had cleaned up her arm and bandaged her. Thanks to her quick reflexes, the wound wasn't as bad as it could have been. Only a handful of stitches were required; the muscle wasn't too severely damaged as the blade hadn't plunged too deep, and Kennedy didn't even need to go to the E.R. to get it sorted.

Once the E.M.T. had given her the all-clear, Kennedy sat and told the police officer everything that happened. She ran over the details of all the places she had seen him and realised that she had noticed him following her for a while. She also thought it best to inform him of Jane's concerns and how the incident could be linked to the murdered judge.

"I'm sorry to have to tell you this, Mrs Daniels, but we lost the suspect," Officer Lancaster said, joining his colleague in the ambulance.

Kennedy smiled back at him weakly and thanked him for his effort, even as her heart began to race at the thought of him still being out there, able to get to her, or worse, Jane.

"If you could please describe the man as best as you can to the sketch artist, we will get a BOLO out of him before the day is out," the officer said, introducing the criminal sketch artist.

Kennedy was furious and in no mood to discuss the matter any further. She was scared and angry, not just at the perp but at herself. She shouldn't have ignored Jane's concerns. Jane had been right. She should have called Arthur and voiced her concerns sooner; perhaps all this mess could have been avoided. Kennedy had no idea why she had questioned Jane's concerns. She had a knack for these things and was never wrong.

Closing her eyes, trying to calm her mind and temper, Kennedy remembered something. Something that could lead to the arrest of such a lunatic. The man who attacked her, they had met before, online. He had tried to contact her several weeks back. He wanted Kennedy's help to hack the police network.

"Just for fun," he had said.

None of this was what Kennedy would class as fun.

"His name is Devon," Kennedy realised.

Kennedy couldn't understand how the situation had gotten so out of hand. How had a simple 'no' turned into a vengeful act that had resulted in the murder of a judge and an attack on her?

"This man is crazy, officer," Kennedy said.

"So, you know him?" asked the officer.

"Not officially. I met him online. He is a first-rate hacker, one of the best I have ever seen. When he asked me to hack the police network, I turned him down and was alerted to his presence again when Detective Inspector Gottfried alerted me to the police network being hacked," Kennedy replied.

"I remember that hacking," the other officer gasped, "we couldn't get back in for days. They had to call some tech wiz to get us back into the network."

"That was me," Kennedy smiled, a hint of pride shooting through her that her reputation proceeded her. "This guy is a wizard at covering his tracks online. I couldn't track him, but I managed to kick him out and block him from re-accessing the network. I only met him in person once before, but I can give you a detailed description," Kennedy answered.

Satisfied that everything had been taken care of at the train station, Kennedy accompanied the officers to their vehicle, mindlessly watching the hustle and bustle of London pass her by from the car window.

Kennedy accompanied the officers back to the station. She finished her description with the sketch artist and filed her statement. Several hours later, feeling calmer but mentally exhausted, Kennedy returned home to find Jane up in arms. As expected, Detective Arthur Gottfried notified Jane of what had occurred.

"What on earth were you doing on the Underground? We have two cars, for crying out loud!" Jane yelled.

"I was taking your suggestion," she laughed nervously, trying to make light of the situation. "My car is booked in next week to get the brakes fixed, and I thought you might need your car today."

"Are you serious? You could have been killed!" Jane yelled, shaking her head in frustration.

Pausing, Jane sighed heavily, launching herself at Kennedy and pulling her into a hug. She never wanted to let her wife out of her sight again. The thought of losing her once was bad enough but twice was almost too much to bear. Kennedy could feel Jane trembling as she gripped her tighter.

"I was so worried," Jane whispered, holding back tears.

Kennedy hugged her wife, comforting her, her heart filled with love for Jane.

"I know, but I'm OK now," Kennedy reassured, taking Jane's face in her hands and staring lovingly into her eyes.

"Arthur is coming over for dinner. He called before you arrived.

They found the guy's flat; it was empty, his computers gone. He has run," Jane said.

Kennedy nodded, shrugging off her jacket and hanging it on the coat rack by the front door.

"I figured as much, but I'm sure I can find him online," Kennedy headed to the kitchen to make herself a much-needed coffee. Being from Boston, she didn't quite understand why everyone in London seemingly loved tea. Kennedy was essentially indifferent to it. She figured that her influence had rubbed off on Jane and Arthur, though, because they nearly always drank coffee.

"What do you mean?"

"Guys like him can't stay offline without logging in somewhere. And when he does, I will find him," Kennedy answered.

Tea in hand, Kennedy turned on her computer with a newfound determination to find her attacker. He had managed to evade her once; she was determined it wouldn't happen again.

It was becoming a bit of a theme; whenever Arthur needed advice about a case, he would always find his way over around dinner time. In all honesty, Kennedy couldn't blame him. Jane was a fantastic cook, as well as a baker. Arthur had made no effort to let them know how much he preferred Jane's cakes to his wife's. A secret he made them both promise to keep.

"And you think this hacker is the same guy who shot the judge?" Arthur asked, blotting his mouth with his napkin.

Jane began to clear the table after their meal, leaving Kennedy to discuss her thoughts with the detective.

"I don't know enough about him to answer that question, Arthur," Kennedy answered. "All I know is he served in Afghanistan and came home two years ago. He said to avoid the nightmares and other symptoms of his P.T.S.D., he went into computer gaming as a distraction."

Arthur nodded, taking it all in, stirring his coffee pensively, "Did he happen to mention what regiment he belonged to?"

"No," Kennedy shook her head. "But I'm guessing if it was a sniper unit, it would make sense that he was the one to shoot the judge."

"I don't know much about specialised units in the army, but I doubt there are many that require both an expert hacker and a sniper. Was he in active combat? Do you think he was an army tech who happened to see some things he wasn't supposed to?" Jane said as she filled their cups with more coffee.

"No, he was definitely in active combat. He went into graphic detail about how he had seen his men gunned down. It was quite alarming," Kennedy admitted.

Jane shot Kennedy a look. *Why didn't she tell me about this?* She felt a pang in her chest. *I trust Kennedy, but I always thought we were honest with each other. She's never kept something this important from me.*

The room fell into an awkward silence. Whoever this man was, he was obviously troubled, skilled, and highly dangerous.

"Do you think he could be coming after Kennedy simply because he knows she knows who he is and can lead the police to him?" Jane asked.

"It's a genuine possibility. No one knows who he is apart from Kennedy. But, on the other hand, he could be trying to tie up any loose ends," Arthur pondered, instantly regretting his choice of words by the concerned looks on both Jane and Kennedy's faces.

CHAPTER 6

On the advice of the police services, Jane and Kennedy locked themselves away at home until the shooter was apprehended. To keep herself occupied, Kennedy searched online for any trace of him, any scrap of information that could aid in his capture. To her surprise, her proactive approach eased Jane's mind. Jane wasn't coping very well with being locked indoors; she missed her job and her routine. She was happy to have time to spend with Kennedy, though.

They spent the long days cuddling on the couch watching boring daytime T.V. and were on track to gain a stone each from eating all the baked goods that resulted from Jane's stress.

After several days of searching, Kennedy had found nothing. He hadn't been online since before the judge's shooting. That doesn't mean Kennedy left empty-handed, thanks to having the last known location of his apartment; thanks to Detective Gottfried, she had his last known I.P. address. With that, she found every Wi-Fi tower his I.P. address had pinged off of over the previous year. She found several locations where he had spent long periods of time, and she handed this over to the police in hopes it would aid them.

Internet cafés, libraries, and other apartment buildings. All very different locations scattered across London. Each site had him logged in for hours. She managed to find a trail of what games he played, what forums he was a part of and all his social media. Some of his posts were alarming, but while Kennedy should have been scared, she felt for the young man. He was in pain, frightened, and alone in the world. He had fought for his country, and everyone had abandoned him.

With only meeting him once until that point, all Kennedy had was Devon's name. Now, she had everything. His full name was Devon Allen Maldin, and he was indeed a sniper in the fifth regiment. Before he joined the army, he had a promising future. He had been accepted to both Oxford and Cambridge and several prestigious universities overseas. His I.Q. was astounding; Kennedy wished she had met him under different circumstances. The things they could learn from each other, the ways they could change the world. The prospect of a future robbed from the world pained Kennedy.

He was a troubled young lad; his lack of medication to help his P.T.S.D. was shocking. And from what Kennedy had found, he hadn't filled his prescription in months or been to any of his scheduled therapy meetings. That said, no one had made any effort to check in on him. His doctors surely must have seen that his medications were not being collected, and his therapist must have noticed when he stopped showing up. So why had no one gone looking for him? Why had the police not been alerted that he was a missing person?

Seeing how troubled Devon Maldin was should have had Kennedy more concerned for her safety, but all it did was make her feel sorry for him. The more information Kennedy found on Devon, the more she wanted to find him. Not to have him arrested, but to help him. The world may have turned its back on Devon, but Kennedy wouldn't.

Almost a month had passed since Devon attacked Kennedy on the London Underground. Jane and Kennedy were starting to go a bit stair crazy being locked up in their home, flinching at every knock on the door, even when they had ordered food. The pair were both on edge.

Around the clock, police surveillance was set up outside their house. It was meant for safety, but the home began to feel more like a prison after a while.

One morning while Jane baked yet another Victoria sponge cake – she had baked so much that Kennedy offered to buy her own bakery once all this Halloween drama was behind them. Kennedy sat at her computer researching P.T.S.D., local charities and organisations, and tech companies getting in on the ground floor with new technology to help recovering veterans with their condition. A gentle knock on the front door startled her.

"It's OK, sweetie; I know that knock. It's Arthur." Jane said, heading to the door to let in their friend.

"Good morning, Jane. Can I have a word with you and Kennedy?" Arthur asked, looking a little grim.

"Of course, head to the kitchen. I will make coffee. You are just in time; I just finished decorating a Victoria sponge cake," Jane smiled.

"My favourite."

"You always did have impeccable timing, Arthur," Kennedy grinned, joining them at the kitchen table.

Kennedy and Arthur made small talk waiting for Jane while she plated up the cake and brought over a fresh pot of coffee, a small pot of sugar cubes and two small jugs, one with milk and the other cream. The coffee smelled strong but not bitter. Jane made the best coffee. It never tasted too strong but wasn't weak, either—a perfect balance.

"So, Arthur, what brings you here so early in the morning?" Jane asked politely, subtly grabbing Kennedy's hand under the table.

"Devon Maldin? We found him," Arthur said before taking a bite of cake.

Kennedy and Jane let out a sigh of relief, releasing a breath they didn't realise they were holding.

"Where did you find him?" Jane asked.

Arthur looked up grimly, regret and sorrow swimming in his gaze. Then, dabbing the edges of his mouth with his napkin, he shook his head softly.

"After we put out the city-wide BOLO, we received a call from some kids in the park between here and the station where he attacked you. Looked like he had been living rough for a while, surviving on scraps found in the bins. It was…. rough," Arthur replied.

"Is he OK?" Kennedy asked, sorrow tugging at her heart.

"He will be, he is getting medical treatment right now, and the police are looking at a rehabilitation centre for P.T.S.D. sufferers," Arthur went quiet, fiddling with his napkin and making several attempts to ask a question he clearly didn't want to ask.

"Spit it out, Gottfried," Kennedy snapped.

"Right… With his current mental state, a judge has deemed him innocent on the grounds of mental incapacity in the judge's shooting. Understandable, due to his state of mind…. however, his attack on you seemed premeditated. I have to ask…do you wish to press charges?"

They shook their heads; they had gone over the pros and cons during their isolation and had decided it wasn't worth potentially ruining someone's opportunity to get help.

"Press charges? How could I? He needs help. Looking back now, I guess he was crying out for help, and I just didn't see it. How could I send that man to prison?" Kennedy asked, troubled.

Standing, she began to pace back and forth across the kitchen. She had vowed she wouldn't turn her back on him like everyone else. She knew that pressing charges wouldn't solve anything. It wouldn't help her sleep at night, and it wouldn't heal her scar or make Jane any less worried. All it would do would stress out an already deeply troubled soul.

"He did try to kill you, Kennedy. Even if he is in prison, I'm sure he will still get the help he needs, right Arthur?" Jane asked.

"Unfortunately, I can't answer that question," Arthur said regretfully. "I'm afraid the noises from prison, the violence we all know goes on behind closed doors yet choose to ignore; it could all act as triggers, and he could end up hurting someone else, or worse, or get himself killed."

"Can I see him? Can I talk to him?" Kennedy asked.

Jane jumped to her feet, alarmed, "You can't be serious?"

"Perhaps if I can speak with him, I could get answers."

"Honestly, Kennedy, what will that do? Will it help him or you?" Arthur asked.

Kennedy looked between her wife and her friend; neither of them understood what she needed. Finally, frustrated and confused, she headed to her office, slamming the door a little harder than intended before locking it tightly.

She spent the rest of the evening scrolling through all of Devon's social media, all of the medical records she could legally access, and any articles about his time in the army. She didn't want to believe a man who was willing to risk his life for the Queen and country could maliciously hurt anyone. Instead, she wanted to try and figure out where exactly the system failed him and what help he would need to get his life back.

Two days passed since they apprehended Devon, and Kennedy had made several attempts to try and see him but was advised against it by the police psychologist. Jane wasn't happy when Kennedy made her decision, but after talking it through, she understood. Kennedy decided that Devon was innocent and just wanted him to get the help he needed.

Kennedy didn't blame him; she didn't pity him either. Instead, she saw what happened as an opportunity for change.

⚮

"Morning sweetie, Arthur just called," Kennedy said, presenting Jane with her breakfast.

"How is he?"

"Good. Devon has been deemed unfit to stand trial. Kennedy answered that the judge thinks he will spend the rest of his days in a mental institution," Kennedy answered.

"Well… that's a sobering thought. But at least he will finally be getting the help he needs. This country has neglected its troop's mental health for far too long. Hopefully, something good comes out of this, and the authorities start to take note, so it doesn't happen again."

Kennedy nodded, not knowing what else to say. Then, heading to the small T.V. on the kitchen counter, she flicked on the news. Good Morning Britain had just finished, and the nine a.m. news was starting. The first report was about Devon.

The news reporter went on to inform the nation how Devon's P.T.S.D. had been left untreated and unmanaged, and as a result, he had spiralled into violent, vengeful outbursts. In addition, he was suffering from panic attacks that were so severe that his vengeance had no boundaries. He was an ill man who needed help.

"This incident has alerted us to the epidemic in this country. We need to pay more attention to our servicemen and women's mental health and safety. They risk their lives to free millions of people from tyranny; they deserve more than a handshake when they arrive home," said the P.T.S.D. charity advocate.

"I couldn't have said it better myself," Kennedy nodded at the screen.

As Kennedy looked around her futuristic, almost fully automated home, her mind wandered. How could technology prevent this from happening in the future? What tech could she help build to stop soldiers from seeing the horrors of war? To eliminate unnecessary loss of life? That's when she decided that would be her new tech venture.

"I kind of feel like this was meant to happen to me," Kennedy pondered.

"How do you mean?" Jane asked.

"I was meant to see the results of human error and use it to create something to help us in the future."

"I think that's wonderful, honey, that you can take something so positive out of a horrible situation. I'm proud of you."

Kennedy hadn't been able to get the news report out of her head for days. Even as Jane prepared for Christmas, which was usually a happy time of year, Kennedy felt she needed to do more. So finally, she decided to reach out to the spokesperson who spoke on Devon's behalf on the news.

She set up a meeting for the New Year. Working with the charity was going to be her new venture. She vowed never to miss the signs of someone needing help again. After speaking with Arthur, he agreed it was an excellent idea; it would be the closure she needed on the incident. And even though she was told, due to the attack, she wouldn't be allowed to work with Devon directly; she was still able to help him. Even in a small way.

"How is he doing?" Jane asked when Kennedy ended her call.

"Slowly but surely," Kennedy replied.

"Did they get any answers on why he shot the judge?"

Kennedy sighed; she knew that Jane wouldn't like the answer.

"He insisted he didn't shoot the judge. He became quite distraught at the thought of it. He said his target was the Scooby-Doo. He said he didn't want the talking dog to interfere with his plans. He even quoted the show, saying how he would have got away with it if it wasn't for the dog and meddling kids. Arthur spoke to some of his old comrades. None of them knew he was suffering, and it seems a harmless prank stayed with him and manifested in nightmares when he got home."

"That's awful," Jane said.

Kennedy waited patiently, knowing it wouldn't be long before Jane put the pieces together.

"Wait! So, his target was... Kennedy...it could have been you he killed!" Jane panicked, "Why did he go after you? Imagine if the judge hadn't been wearing the same costume."

"No point in speculating on what could have happened. It doesn't help anyone. Apparently, when I refused to help him hack the police network, it triggered the 'baffoon' trying to stop his fun," Kennedy shrugged.

"Don't do that," Jane said softly, wrapping her arms around her wife.

"Do what?"

"I know that look. You are blaming yourself. How could you have known this is what would happen?"

Kennedy nodded; she knew Jane was right. She had done some research online, concerned about how she was feeling. Psychologists called it survivor's guilt. Kennedy realised that now, she and Devon had much more in common than just being good with a computer.

"A hunted house, a man haunted by the ghosts of his past. A life lost. I bet Mayor Porter never intended for her Halloween Ball to be so...."

"Memorable? In the worst possible way."

"Exactly."

"Well, I think it's safe to say this Halloween was one to remember," Jane sighed.

"One I would rather forget; now, let us start looking forward to Christmas," Kennedy smiled.

The following day, Jane sat curled up in a ball on the sofa, wrapped in what Kennedy knew was Jane's thinking blanket. Like a comforter from her childhood, a blanket her great grandmother had made.

Kennedy peaked around the living room door watching with a smile on her face. Jane smiled, stirring her hot chocolate, another tell of hers that Jane had picked up on over the years.

"What are you thinking?" Kennedy asked, joining Jane on the sofa and wrapping her arms around her.

"I was thinking about the trick or treaters we missed....and all the other things we could have missed if things had ended differently...."

"Baby, I've told you not to worry...."

"Please let me finish," Jane interrupted softly, "I then started thinking about how you took something positive out of the horrors of the night. I've been thinking about something for a while now, and I wanted to discuss it with you."

Jane paused, and Kennedy could feel she was shaking, nervous. Kennedy kissed her head and stroked her hair, reassuring her she could talk to her about anything.

"It's OK, baby; talk to me."

"I think it's time we...."

"Have a baby?"

Jane sat up, surprised by Kennedy's response. It was as if she had read her mind.

"Yes," Jane stuttered.

"I've been thinking about it too. Even in the tiniest way, I guess facing death makes you re-evaluate what's important. While I love my job and helping Arthur, I found the part of Halloween I missed the most was the kids. It's something you have wanted for a while, and don't think I haven't noticed how you put your dreams aside for me. Now I think we are ready."

"So... we... are going to start looking into having a kid?" Jane grinned.

Kennedy smiled a nodded back.

"I love you so much," Jane breathed, tears causing her eyes to glisten like stars as she flung her arms around Kennedy.

"Even though we are closer to Christmas now, I feel like this all resulted from Halloween. What was it you said yesterday?"

"A Halloween to remember," Jane smiled.

"A Halloween to remember," Kennedy winked.

The End

DEAD MAN DALTON

A PINE GROVE MYSTERY

PROLOGUE

M r. Dalton sat in his armchair, stroking the barrel of his shotgun. He hadn't loaded it yet, but knowing it was there gave him a sense of comfort.

The sound of the TV gently hummed as Mr. Dalton lowered it to almost mute. With the subtitles on, he didn't need the sound on. But he found he couldn't sit comfortably in his home in silence. Loneliness was a terrible thing, and he was afraid of what lurked in the shadows around his house.

The fireplace gently warmed the room, casting shadows of orange across the dirty, unkempt rug that hadn't been vacuumed in over a year. Then, finally, the soft crackle of the ember's lulled Mr. Dalton, and his eyes fluttered shut.

Suddenly, his eyes snapped open, and he could hear rustling in the bush at the back of his house, a sound he had become accustomed to – A sound he wished would go away. Someone was out there….again.

Mr. Dalton couldn't remember when it started, but he should have known it would. You can never outrun your past, no matter how hard you try. The guilt had eaten at him for years, and Mr. Dalton often wondered if this was karma, a payback he deserved.

Turning off the lamp on the side table next to his chair, he picked up the gun and slowly crept to the back door. Pushing the small fabric that covered the square glass window, he peeked outside, hands shaking, causing the gun to rattle. He had forgotten he hadn't loaded it; the shells sat next to the lamp in the other room.

This is my home. They will not make me run from my home! Mr. Dalton vowed.

Taking several deep breaths to calm his nerves, he pushed the door open with such force that it slammed against the outside wall, startling birds in the trees and causing them to take flight.

"Go away! Leave me alone! This is your final warning; do you hear me? Next time you will meet the business end of my shotgun! I will kill you; I promise you that!" Mr. Dalton yelled.

His words echoed into the night. Mr. Dalton stood waiting, listening. Searching the blackness of the woods surrounding his home, Mr. Dalton saw nothing, which was unsurprising since his eyesight wasn't what it used to be. Was that a shadow on the porch or a figment of his imagination?

A cold fall wind pushed through the trees, sending a shiver down the old man's spine. After waiting a little longer and finally satisfied he had scared away whoever stalked his home, Mr. Dalton stormed back inside, slamming the door, muttering to himself.

"Know what you did...I did....my house! It's my house! My Sylvia."

The old man's terrified voice rang through the trees. The simplest of acts was having the desired effect; Mr. Dalton seemed positively unhinged. Revenge was sweet. The old man would pay.

It appeared that Mr. Dalton might shoot for a second, but concern faded when his shaking hands rattled the empty gun.

The old fool must have forgotten to load it.

The plan was reaching its end, it wouldn't be long now. But first, a trap must be set. The old man must be seen as crazy; that way, it would look less suspicious.

The old man had made that part of the job easy. From the cover of the trees, lights could be seen flickering to life in the houses next door.

That's right old man, scream and shout. Let it all out. You are digging your own grave.

CHAPTER 1

ctober, New England

O The leaves from trees decorated the parking lot in shades of browns, oranges, and reds, giving a satisfying crunch underfoot. Peter Myers pushed his shopping cart around the store. Fall in New England was the perfect time for soups, casseroles, and other comfort foods. But sausage casserole wouldn't be sufficient for the meal he had planned. This was no ordinary meal; it was a first date with the beautiful, kind, always smiling Dr. Jessica, the vet.

For some reason, she had implanted herself in Peter's mind ever since she helped Peter out with Sam. And Sam swiftly gave him an excuse to see her again when he hurt his paw out on a morning run with Peter. So, the pair met again as if it were fate – or canine intervention – and Peter seized his chance to ask her out.

The date was set for the following evening, giving Peter enough time to calm his nerves and straighten the house. Jessica was coming around for dinner, so it had to be special. Grabbing a few steaks and extra for Sam, red wine, and a cheesecake, Peter walked to the checkout desk with a smile and a spring in his step.

"That everything?" Leah asked, not paying attention.

Even after a month's return, Peter still found how much Leah had changed. Whenever he went for groceries, it was clear that Leah wanted to be anywhere else but the store.

"That's everything. Thanks, Leah," Peter smiled, handing over the cash.

Leah grunted something that resembled acknowledgment and shrugged as she handed Peter his change and stuffed his shopping into brown paper bags. Peter bid Leah farewell and headed to his car, groceries in hand. With every step closer, his mind raced with thoughts of Jessica and the excitement of the evening to come.

Peter was not usually the type to listen to music in the car, but this was a special occasion. Fiddling with the radio to find the perfect station, Peter began to reverse out of his parking spot when he was suddenly and forcefully shot forward. His head tapped the staring wheel, dazing and confusing him momentarily.

Quickly checking himself over the rearview mirror, Peter was pleased to find he wasn't hurt, just a little surprised. He was sure he had been paying attention and hadn't seen anything coming when he reversed his vehicle. Then, startled by guilt and concern raging in the pit of his stomach, Peter jumped from his truck to find his old science teacher Mr. Dalton.

Mr. Dalton looked like he had seen better days. His hair had long since thinned and was white from old age. With unkempt hair and clothes that looked a little worse for wear, Mr. Dalton looked back at Peter, dazed and just as startled. Startlement turned to anger, and the old man's face turned red with rage.

"Look what you did! Look! My groceries are ruined! This is your fault! Why were you not watching where you were going?" Mr. Dalton screamed at Peter, wagging a finger as he strode closer.

Peter glanced at where the two cars had collided. Both bumpers were scratched and badly dented with smashed rear headlights. Yet, the only thing that concerned Mr. Dalton was his groceries. Looking at the back window, Peter could see why Mr. Dalton was angry. Eggs leaked from the carton, milk poured over the back seats, and a few other pieces lay askew.

"I'm so sorry, Mr. Dalton, I didn't see you when I reversed. You must have been in my blind spot. I will pay for the damage to the car, of course...." Peter began.

It was hard not to notice how, since a small gathering of on-lookers had appeared, Mr. Dalton had become visibly distressed. His hands shook, he fidgeted with the hem of his jacket, and his eyes darted around the crowd. Then, interrupting Peter's apology, Mr. Dalton began to scream again.

"I don't care about that! Just move your car. I want to go home! Now! Move!"

"Please allow me to replace your groceries before you go," Peter insisted.

"I said I don't care! I want to go home! Move your car before I get in it and move it for you!" Mr. Dalton roared, his face growing red and flustered.

An older lady with a yappy little dog, who hadn't stopped barking at Mr. Dalton since he began yelling, stepped forward. Scooping her frightened pooch into her arms like a child, she gently tapped Peter on the shoulder.

"Do you want me to call the police for you?" she asked.

"No! No! No! Just move! And get that dog to shut its trap!" Mr. Dalton yelled.

He seemed even more agitated since the police were mentioned. The old lady gasped and took several steps back, clinging to her canine companion for dear life.

Concerned but not wanting to push the old man further, Peter nodded and reluctantly moved his vehicle. Then, stepping out, Peter watched as Mr. Dalton continued to scan the crowd before jumping in and speeding off, almost running a red light as he tore down the street.

Turning back to the store, Peter saw Leah leaning against the wall outside, cigarette in hand, staring blankly into the distance.

"Hey, Leah. What's wrong with Mr. Dalton?" Peter asked.

She took one last drag and blew out a cloud of smoke, tossing her butt on the floor and crushing it with her boot. Leah shrugged before heading back inside.

CHAPTER 2

Myers' Residence

Sitting in the backyard with Sam resting on his feet, Peter tried to read the paper for several minutes. But all he could think about was the events from earlier that day. Perhaps he had been distracted thinking about Jessica or tapping along with the radio for the accident to be partially his fault. He racked his mind and was sure he had checked his rearview, side mirrors, and blind spot before reversing.

But that wasn't the only thing that plagued Peter's mind. Mr. Dalton had looked shabbier than Peter had ever seen him. Peter thought back to when Mr. Dalton was his science teacher; he was always a man who took pride in his appearance and had expensive tastes regarding clothes, especially his shoes. Peter worried about poor old Mr. Dalton. How he shifted uneasily and panicked around the small crowd of on-lookers wasn't the strong-minded Mr. Dalton Peter remembered.

"Was it the crowd or the fact someone offered to call the police?" Peter asked.

"Woof," Sam barked softly to answer Peter's question.

"Yeah, Mr. Dalton might not have insurance. You are right, boy," Peter muttered, stroking Sam on the head.

If Mr. Dalton didn't have insurance and had let himself go a bit, perhaps he was in financial trouble. Guilt pooled in Peter's stomach. If the old man was having money issues, Peter had just ruined possibly a month worth of food that couldn't be replaced. Peter couldn't sit back and let a man he respected go hungry, not when he had the means to help.

"No, I can't sit back and do nothing," Peter said. Grabbing his coat, wallet, and keys, he headed back to the store.

With the help of Tiff, Peter's trusted agent friend; it didn't take long for Peter to have the correct address for his old science teacher. Pulling up to the street, Peter sighed. Unfortunately, not all the houses were numbered; it would be tricky to find exactly which house was the right one.

"What are you looking for, friend?" came a woman's voice from a house across the street. She was poking her head out of the window.

Peter swiftly deduced that this person, whoever she was, was the street's nosey neighbor. Every street had one, after all.

"I'm looking for Mr. Dalton's house," Peter replied, unpacking the groceries from the car.

"That one there, with the messy lawn," pointed the woman as she closed the blinds and headed back inside.

Turning, it was apparent which house she was referring to. All the other lawns were mowed to perfection, lush and green with a few sprinklings of autumn leaves. However, Mr. Dalton's yard was at least four feet high and dead, the paint on the outside of his house had long flaked off, and the redwood door was in disrepair.

Strolling up to the front door, Peter set the groceries down on the front porch, stood, and prepared to knock when crazed ramblings grew louder from the other side.

"Get off my property!" came Mr. Dalton's voice.

Suddenly the door flew open. Standing in the doorway was Mr. Dalton brandishing a shotgun.

"Get off my porch! Go away! Leave me alone!" Mr. Dalton yelled, waving the shotgun in Peter's direction.

Thinking fast, Peter took several steps back, raising his hands above his head. Heart pounding, Peter kept his eyes locked on the barrel of the gun.

CHAPTER 3

alton Residence
D "Mr. Dalton, please, I only came to replace the groceries I damaged earlier on," Peter said, trying to calm the situation.

"I told you I didn't care about that! Don't you youngsters listen?"

Peter chuckled internally; it had been a few years since anyone referred to him as a youngster. But in comparison to Mr. Dalton, the old man wasn't entirely wrong. Mr. Dalton was close to eighty years old, at least. Time had aged his features, and age-related spots decorated his face.

"Mr. Dalton, please. Put the gun down," Peter said softly.

"It's my first amendment right to bear arms. I'm protecting myself; now go before I shoot. This is your final warning!" Mr. Dalton yelled cocking the gun with a telltale clink.

"All right, I'm leaving," Peter admitted defeat.

There was no talking sense into the old man. He was simply crotchety and mean, trodden on by life that had dampened his spirits. Not wanting to agitate the old man any further, Peter walked back slowly to his car, keeping a close eye on the shaking gun aimed directly at him. Getting into his car, Peter sighed deeply before slowly driving away.

Peter didn't fully know why, but even with the growing wind of October, he ended up sitting outside a café on the town's main strip. Of course, it made more sense to sit inside. But as Pine Grove had changed so much since he was last there, Peter decided to people-watch. Images raced through his thoughts. He thought about Leah, what she was like in high school and who she was now. Marconi crossed his mind and all the drama of the previous month. And finally, Mr. Dalton.

It saddened Peter to see his old teacher in such a way. Questions spun in his mind. Did Mr. Dalton have anyone to care for him? What had happened to make him so on edge? And more importantly, had he ever hurt anyone with that shotgun? Peter worried that with a weapon of such caliber and in his nervous state, Mr. Dalton might wind up hurting himself or someone else.

Peter remembered Mr. Dalton's science classes fondly. Mr. Dalton spoke of science with such passion that even the unruliest student was enthralled by his words. He took a potentially complicated and boring subject and made it fun. To his students, Mr. Dalton was a hero, a superhero. Mr. Dalton once commanded a room; people had stopped and listened. And now, the poor man seemed to cower at the world. It broke Peter's heart to see a man he always respected reduced to a fragment of the man he used to be.

His eyes followed the bustling crowd of people pulling their coats tighter around themselves, guarding against the wind. The leaves found new homes around town, scattering the streets as cars zoomed past. Peter's eyes fell on Leah coming out of the post office next door. He hadn't noticed her go in, and he had been sitting outside for so long that his coffee had gone cold.

"Hey Leah, do you have a minute?" Peter called, waving Leah over.

Shrugging, Leah joined him at the table.

"What's up? I'm a bit busy," Leah said.

"I won't keep you long, I promise. I was just curious, what's Mr. Dalton's story? Unfortunately, he isn't as I remember him."

Pulling a cigarette from her purse and lighting it, Leah took a long drag, blowing the smoke away from Peter, which drifted back his way with the wind. Then, shrugging, she tightened her scarf around her neck.

"I'm not sure of the full story, but he retired a few years ago. From what I remember, it was health issues, and there was a big stink about it, too," Leah answered.

"Stink? How so?"

"It wasn't his decision."

"He was forced to retire?" Peter asked for clarification.

Leah nodded, taking another long drag.

"Forget about him; he is a nutcase. Neighbors say they can hear him arguing with himself. And a few times, he has come out of his house waving that damn shotgun around. It wouldn't surprise me if he killed someone or himself," Leah said.

"I see," Peter said.

"I mean, everyone knows he has money, so why is he suddenly acting like he is poor? It is beyond me. As I said, nutcase," Leah said, finishing her cigarette, "Anyway, I got to go."

"One more thing, please. What was his health issue?"

"Some sort of mental breakdown, I think, I don't know," Leah shrugged, hooking her bag over her shoulder and leaving Peter with his thoughts.

Peter disagreed with Leah. Peter didn't believe Mr. Dalton was a nutcase. If anything, Leah's observations only drew more concern. Something didn't add up. There was a missing piece to the puzzle. An academic like Mr. Dalton wouldn't just shift overnight. And for someone who took his career as seriously as he did, for him to be forced to retire said something was wrong. From what Peter could remember, Mr. Dalton always hated guns, but now a shotgun appeared to be his companion.

Is Mr. Dalton afraid of something? Of course, the biggest unanswered question was why he was so scared.

CHAPTER 4

Myers' Residence

It was surprisingly calm for an October morning, with a slight chill in the air but nothing bad enough to put Peter off his morning jog.

"Come on, boy, time for some exercise," Peter said, holding the door open.

"Woof, Woof," Sam replied, charging off ahead.

Peter chuckled to himself, gently jogging after Sam through the woods surrounding the property. The weather wasn't cold enough to warrant frost, but Peter knew it would be a harsh winter from the crushing underfoot. New England was beautiful in the fall. Peter admired the scenery as he ran, taking in all the sights, sounds, and smells of fall. So gorgeous; no other word would suffice.

"Come on, boy, time to head home," Peter said, turning off the trail.

Peter had recently changed his morning jog route. He started through the trail at the back and headed around the neighborhood. He waved good morning to the few people awake at that time of day. Then, he finished his run at the front of his house.

"Woof!" Sam barked swiftly, following suit.

As Peter jogged up the gravel path outside his house, he saw a sight he wasn't expecting. Parked outside his house was a police car. One officer sat inside, visibly scrolling on his form, while the other stood leaning against the vehicle.

Sam stopped, offering a low growl in warning.

"Shush, Sam, it's all right," Peter soothed.

"Morning officers, how can I help?" Peter asked, opening the door and letting Sam run inside.

"Peter Myers?" asked the officer leaning against the car.

"That's me," Peter answered.

"We need you to come to the police station," said the officer whose name stood proudly embroidered above his badge. Officer Samson.

"What is this regarding?" Peter asked.

"Mr. Dalton was found dead this morning, and our sources say you were the last person to see him alive," Officer Samson said, his fingers fiddling with the handcuffs on his hip.

It was hard for Peter not to let his eyes drift to the loosely veiled threat. Was he under arrest? Was he being asked to come in voluntarily, or had Sam picked up on a bad vibe Peter had missed?

"Am I under arrest, officer?" Peter asked.

Sam, sensing the growing tension, popped his head out the door. Standing guard, he let out a low growl, standing close to Peter's hip.

"Quiet, Sam," Peter said, gently stroking the dog's head.

"You are not under arrest. No, we want you to come with us to answer some questions. A neighbor's video cam puts you at the crime scene. I believe you are a lawyer, so you understand the law," Officer Samson replied, his eyes not leaving Sam, who still stood offering soft growls.

"I understand. Let me lock up, and I'll be right with you," Peter offered.

Reluctantly, Sam went inside, jumping at Peter as if trying to convince him to stay. Peter didn't like locking Sam up in the kitchen, even if it was spacious enough for him. Usually, Sam had free roam the house while he was out. But Peter could sense Sam's anxiety at the police presence and needed to keep him calm.

"Sorry, boy, but you will have to stay here. Drink, rest; I'll be back soon," Peter said, closing the kitchen door behind him.

Sam barked in protest; his claws scratching at the door could be heard throughout the house. Soft whimpers followed Peter as he walked to the front door, pulling at Peter's heartstrings. Peter waited at the front door for Sam to quiet before leaving and heading to the police station with the officers.

CHAPTER 5

ine Grove Police Station
    Walking through the police station, Peter walked with his head held high. He knew he was innocent and would not let the officers trying to intimidate him. Peter was a good lawyer and knew the law; he also knew evidence would prove him innocent.

Officer Samson directed him to a small interrogation room at the back of the station, no different from the rooms Peter had sat in before with his clients. He knew he would be left there for a while to stew, a poor effort to make him nervous. But Peter was calm, relaxed, and waiting. Sitting in the purposefully uncomfortable plastic chair, Peter sat with his hands clasped in front of him on the desk. The sound of the station was ringing through the door.

Finally, Officer Samson returned with the police captain. It was the captain Peter met during the mayor's case only a month ago. Peter got the same feeling then as he did now; something was off about the captain. Peter just didn't know what. But Peter knew if anyone could find out what that man was doing, it would be him, all in good time.

"So, Mr. Myers...."

"Peter, please," Peter interrupted.

Peter was not the type to interrupt people; he found it rude. But he wanted to let them know he wouldn't be intimidated at that moment.

"Of course....Peter. Where were you last night?" the captain asked.

"What time specifically?" Peter asked.

The captain exchanged a look with Officer Samson. Either they didn't have an accurate time of death, or they were not expecting Peter to ask his own questions.

"I'm asking the questions here, Mr. Myers. We have footage putting you at the crime scene," the captain said, opening a folder.

Inside sat a screenshot of Peter leaving Mr. Dalton's house. From what Peter could see, it was just before he drove off. He remembered it well.

"So I've been told," Peter said, his eyes flashing to Officer Samson.

"Why were you at the Dalton residence?" the captain asked.

"I had a run-in with Mr. Dalton earlier that day. We had a small crash in the parking lot at the grocery store. He seemed shaken up and complained that I had spoilt his groceries. I felt for him, so I went to deliver new ones. The footage you have will show me dropping them off. When I arrived, he made it clear he didn't want me there, so I left," Peter said, folding his arms across his chest.

"Yes, we have footage of you leaving," Officer Samson said.

"So, officers, tell me. If you have footage of me leaving, why am I here? The footage will show that I left swiftly after I arrived."

The officers exchanged a look once more before Officer Samson, who seemed less intimidating than earlier that morning, continued.

"A neighbor called in the incident. They were leaving for work when they saw Mr. Dalton's door ajar. When they went in to investigate, they found him dead. Looks like blunt force trauma to the head. His skull was in pieces on the floor. When we arrived, they offered up their doorbell footage as evidence."

"So....what happened to the footage from the rest of the day? Because I arrived at Mr. Dalton's house just after one o'clock in the afternoon and left all of five minutes later with Mr. Dalton very much alive, waving a shotgun in my direction," Peter said.

"Yes, we are aware of Mr. Dalton and his gun," Samson offered.

"Officer Samson, will you examine the footage at the time Mr. Myers mentioned? Then, I shall continue the interview," Donnelly said.

Peter sat button-lipped, watching Officer Samson leave. Officer Donnelly seemed visibly annoyed when Officer Samson gave Peter details of the case. Perhaps getting rid of him was the officer's way of keeping information from Peter.

"Look, officer...."

"Captain, actually," Donnelly gave a sly smile.

Peter fought not to roll his eyes, offering a soft smile.

"Apologies....Captain Donnelly, I had nothing to do with this. I brought Mr. Dalton groceries and nothing more. I assure you that the time of death will clear up my involvement. Do you have any more questions for me, or am I free to leave?" Peter asked.

The captain glared at Peter silently before closing the folder and tucking it under his arm.

"You are free to go....for now. We will wait on the results of the autopsy. But do not leave town, or I will arrest you for perverting the course of justice," the captain said while he stood.

"I wouldn't dream of it, officer....sorry, captain," Peter said.

As Peter headed home, his mind went into overdrive. The captain hadn't offered any information about how exactly Mr. Dalton had passed, what time, or even asked many questions. Was he expecting a confession there and then? Purely based on some grainy doorbell footage? What was the captain up to? Was he trying to use Peter as a scapegoat? Either way, Peter knew from the investigation with the mayor that the captain's police work was not up to scratch. If Peter wanted answers, he would have to find them himself.

CHAPTER 6

His frustration grew; Peter didn't like being kept in the dark. Too many questions were left unanswered. If the police had footage of Peter leaving, where was the footage? Why had they not considered that he wasn't covered in blood? Peter had seen enough crime scene photos over the years to know a thing or two about blood splatter in a case like this.

I think it's time to do a little investigation of my own, Peter thought, heading home to collect his car and to see Mr. Dalton's nosey neighbors. Arriving at Mr. Dalton's street, Peter pulled up and scanned the houses across the street for a video doorbell. Three had them, but with a familiar face poking out of the window, it was easy for Peter to deduce which house the footage had come from. The name on the letter box said *Logan,* and from what Peter had seen at the station, which meant the Taylor who had handed in the footage was a woman. Peter remembered seeing the witness' name on the folder before the police captain pulled it away. Another instance of the police chief's sloppy police work – Never let a murder suspect know any details about potential eyewitnesses.

Locking eyes with Peter, the woman who directed him to Mr. Dalton's house only the day before swiftly closed the curtains and rushed inside. It appeared she was the type to be in everyone's business. Peter strode to the door and pressed the large blue circular light on the doorbell. He waited patiently for a moment before a woman opened the door.

"Hello, Taylor Logan, is it? I'm Peter. I was wondering if I could borrow a moment of your time to ask about Mr. Dalton?" Peter smiled softly.

"I know who you are. If you don't leave, I'm calling the police," she insisted.

Peter looked Taylor over for a woman just sitting at home staring out and spying on the neighbors. She was dressed as if she was about to go out for drinks with the girls. The telltale red bottoms of her shoes that lay on the floor in the hall beside her bare feet screamed Louboutin. Her dress and jacket were clearly designer too. She held herself with a level of self-confidence and arrogance, folding her arms across her chest and resting her shoulder against the door frame. A smug look of superiority spread across her face.

"How do you know who I am if you only saw my car?" Peter challenged.

Taylor looked back at Peter, visibly startled with wide eyes. His statement made it clear that he had seen the footage she handed to the police, and she wasn't expecting to be interrogated, not at her doorstep. Peter waited for a response, silently letting Taylor know he wasn't going anywhere without answers.

"I saw you with my own eyes," she muttered, her eyes falling to the ground.

"I mean no harm, Mrs. Logan. I only want to ask a few questions; then I will leave you to your day," Peter said.

"I don't have to answer your questions! I know what you did! Now go away!" Mrs. Logan snapped, her voice raising in volume.

"Who is that at the door?" growled a croaky dry voice from inside the house.

Loud pounding footsteps echoed through the hall behind the door.

"Who is making all that noise?"

Suddenly, the door swung open. Peter was face-to-face with his old school buddy, Greg Logan. Peter couldn't believe he hadn't recognized the name sooner. How could he forget Greg Logan? Greg was once the school's star athlete but had since let himself go. His hair was thinning on top of his head, and his white tank top was food-stained, stretching over a large beer belly. Peter could see in Greg's eyes that he was half drunk. And for only eleven in the morning, it was concerning. A half drank bottle swayed in Greg's hand as he wiped his mattered beard with his other hand.

When Greg caught sight of Peter, his entire demeanor changed, as did Taylor's at her husband's arrival. Peter couldn't help but notice how she shrank when Greg raised his voice and how she appeared to cower when the door ripped open. This was obviously not a happy household. Was Greg an angry drunk? Had he killed Mr. Dalton while Taylor tried to frame Peter to protect her husband?

"Peter? Man, I haven't seen you in years. How have you been, buddy? Come here," Greg said, his face lighting up in a smile.

Pushing past his wife, Greg pulled a reluctant Peter into a hug. Greg's smell filled Peter's nostrils, and Peter struggled to keep his face vacant. Body odor, cigarette smoke, and beer were just a few of Greg's foul smells. This, a shocking contrast to the woman who stood over his shoulder, a woman who took pride in her appearance compared to her husband, who seemed to no longer care about his. Stained leftover food stuck to his mattered beard. Peter forced a smile.

"Good to see you, Greg," Peter lied, taking a small step back.

"What brings you to my place?" Greg asked, taking a swig of his beer.

"I've just come to ask Taylor about Mr. Dalton, see if I can shed some light on the situation," Peter answered.

"Oh yeah, right, you're a big fancy lawyer now, huh? Don't mind Taylor. She is always up in everyone's business and gets worked up about stupid things," Greg said, waving a dismissive hand in Taylor's direction.

Taylor clearly didn't like being dismissed and suddenly stood up straighter with a defiant look.

"Well, I don't think murder is stupid. That's why I handed the footage to the police," Taylor said proudly, as though she deserved a Nobel prize for citizen of the year.

Greg scoffed, waving another dismissive hand at his wife.

"Oh pish, Mr. Dalton was an old fool. No one murdered him. He probably slipped and bashed his head in on the stairs. We all know he was going crazy. Why do you think the school fired him in the first place?" Greg said, his half-drink state loosening his tongue.

"Fired? I heard he was forced to retire?" Peter enquired.

"Isn't that the same thing?" Greg laughed, his overly large belly jiggling as he did.

"Right," Peter said, about to give up.

Between Taylor refusing to give up information, she had already decided that Peter was guilty, and Greg's drunken state Peter wasn't going to find the answer he was hoping for. Preparing to leave and look for solutions elsewhere, Peter nodded softly and turned to go when something Greg said startled not just him but Taylor too.

"Or who knows, maybe that no good son of his finally did him in," Greg blurted out, stumbling and bashing his back against the door frame.

Taylor gasped, "I went to school with Todd. He wouldn't do such a thing," Taylor protested.

"Why are you so concerned all of a sudden?" Greg snapped at Taylor.

"I'm not; you just caught me off guard. I've had enough of this conversation now anyway," Taylor stormed off back inside, but Peter could see she had set up camp by the window, prepared to watch him leave.

Peter could sense that there was more to it than Taylor was admitting. Why else would she act so shocked by the accusation? Drunken words are sober thoughts. After all, perhaps Greg was speaking some sense. Peter decided that maybe a change in subject would offer more insight.

"Wow, anyway, Greg, how have you been? Last time I saw you, you were on track for a football scholarship," Peter said, slipping into buddy mode.

"Nah, busted my knee final year, didn't I? Oh well, what can you do, hey? Been working at the car dealership outside Pine Grove for years now," Greg said.

"You always did have a thing for cars," Peter chuckled.

"Yeh, but I was laid off a few months ago now. I don't know what else to do. The dealership had been my life," Greg muttered.

The atmosphere grew tense and solemn. Greg's eyes looked like they were glistening with tears. A man broken by life and struggling with his pride and failed dreams. Downing the rest of his drink in one gulp, Greg tossed the empty bottle onto the lawn outside his house. It was plain for all to see that, as a way to deal with his broken childhood dream, Greg had chosen a life of drowning his sorrows.

"Anyway, Peter, good to see you. We should meet for drinks some-time, have a guy's night for the old days," Greg said, running his hands over his face but keeping his gaze away from Peter.

"Sure, Greg, sounds good," Peter said, pity filling him seeing Greg's state.

"Cool, man, cool," Greg muttered, heading back inside.

Both men knew they would never meet up for drinks, but Peter worried that perhaps all Greg needed was a friend. Dissatisfied that he was no closer to figuring things out, Peter put his sights on other things. He still had his date with Jessica later that evening, and that was something he was much looking forward to.

CHAPTER 7

yers' residence

Jessica arrived just after six. She came straight from work, still wearing her white lab coat. Peter didn't mind, she still looked beautiful, and her smile lit up the room. The first course was a shrimp salad, which went down like a treat with the white wind Jessica brought along. Sam was defiantly happy to see her.

At first, Peter had to fight for Jessica's attention. Sam jumped all over her, licking her face and jumping in her lap for hugs. Peter struggled to get Sam to stop trying to join them at the table, shooing him off the spare seat several times and making Jessica laugh. Her laugh was warm, and it felt like a hug had filled the room. Peter never expected to feel a rush like it, but things with Jessica seemed so easy. Their conversation flowed and was never dull. But it wasn't long before the talk of the town buzz popped up.

News traveled fast in Pine Grove, and Taylor Logan had helped by fanning the flames and whispers. Soon the entire town was talking about Peter Myers, the big-shot lawyer now being investigated for murder.

Peter slapped three steaks on the grill, and Sam was swift on his heels. Slathering, knowing one of those juicy stakes was for him.

"Sam, calm down, boy," Peter insisted.

"Woof," Sam barked, his tail wagging manically.

"Sam," Jessica said, clicking her fingers.

Sam bounced across the room, happy to sit proudly at Jessica's side while she sipped her wine.

"He likes you. He responds well to you, too," Peter smiled.

"Well, the feeling is mutual, buddy," Jessica said to Sam, who barked back happily.

"I'm curious, how does someone like you get the town so a buzz?" Jessica asked, stroking the stem of her wine glass.

"Someone like me? I don't know if I should take that as an insult or a compliment," Peter joked.

"You know what I mean, someone so put together. I can't remember the last time someone set tongues wagging so much," Jessica laughed.

Peter appreciated that she was trying to make a joke out of the situation; it made it easier. Even though Peter knew he was innocent, he couldn't help but feel somewhat nervous. The police captain clearly had no clue what he was doing and was set on pinning the murder on Peter. There was also the fact that he couldn't get any sense out of Greg and Taylor, and with every rumor that met his ears, more questions arose. It appeared Taylor had spun enough of a tale around town that everyone had painted Peter as the villain: The sell-out who left town and came back only to murder a much-loved, innocent old teacher.

"The tongues wagging didn't stop you from coming for dinner," Peter pointed out.

"Maybe I'm curious if you killed the old man," Jessica laughed, giving Peter a little wink.

"What if I did? Are you not worried about what people might think of you choosing to dine with a murderer?" Peter asked.

"No. Some other news will pique their curiosity soon enough, and the vet's practice has been crazy lately, so even if business slows, I could use the break," Jessica said.

Peter shrugged in understanding.

"I'd be more worried about being murdered too, but ok," Peter mocked.

Jessica laughed, her laugh warming Peter's heart.

"IF you were going to kill me, I think you would have done it already," Jessica teased.

There was no avoiding the conversation. Avoidance would only make him look guilty. And Peter had nothing to hide. Jessica had been living in Pine Grove for the last few years, and the way gossip spread through the town, it would make sense that if anyone knew something about Mr. Dalton, Jessica would, especially since Peter had been out of town for so many years.

"Do you know anything about Mr. Dalton's son?" Peter asked.

He had tried digging but couldn't find much information on the wayward son. Taylor's reaction made his gut twist, thinking perhaps the son was more involved than he thought. What if Taylor and Dalton's son had an affair, and Mr. Dalton had found out? That would be motive enough for murder. Mr. Dalton could have threatened to tell Greg.

Jessica shook her head, taking another sip of wine.

"I didn't really know either of them, to be honest. I didn't go to school here, so I only know Mr. Dalton as the crabby old man who mumbles around town, or so the rumors call him. I always thought it was a cruel way to describe someone. Although, I did hear an owner of one of my patients say that Mr. Dalton's son is in town," Jessica realized.

"Really?" Peter asked, his curiosity piqued.

"Yeah, I remember now. They were talking to my boss. They said they were surprised he got here so quickly, considering he lives in Oregon. He works at a college or something, maybe as a teaching assistant or a sports coach? I can't exactly remember. But I remember thinking, it's the middle of the academic year. How could he leave like that?" Jessica answered, shrugging.

"Good point."

"Anyway, I can't imagine you invited me around to talk about the investigation, so how about a subject change?" Jessica offered.

"That would be greatly appreciated, thank you," Peter smiled.

The rest of the night went better than Peter had expected. With Jessica having patients early in the morning, she didn't stay too late, but that didn't mean the night wasn't fun. Being a gentleman, Peter didn't venture for a goodnight kiss. He respected Jessica and wanted the chance to get to know her better first. Everything he had seen so far, he liked. She was funny, strong-minded, and didn't care for idle gossip. Sam loved her, and she him. But even as his mind raced with thoughts of the evening, Jessica telling him Dalton's son was in town occupied his thoughts.

CHAPTER 8

alton Residence

D   Peter tried to rest, tossing and turning, knowing Mr. Dalton's murder needed an answer. Then, unable to leave well enough alone, He dressed in an all-black tracksuit and baseball cap and headed out.

"Woof!" Sam barked.

"Sorry, boy, you can't come with me. But I'll be back soon," Peter said, offering Sam a treat.

Peter parked around the corner from Mr. Dalton's house. He didn't want to be spotted by the fancy new doorbell camera. Creeping through the shrubbery around the house, Peter checked windows and doors. No one appeared to be inside, which was not surprising. Then, sneaking out back through the woods, using the torch on his phone, Peter searched for any clues that someone may have broken in or come out.

Bedded deep in the flower bed were boot prints, two sets. One was likely Mr. Dalton's, but to whom did the others belong? Peter followed the larger pair that traveled around the house, close to all the windows. Someone was watching Mr. Dalton.

Looks like the old man wasn't crazy after all. The poor guy was scared, and rightly so, Peter thought, heading to the back of the house.

If there were enough clues out the back that Peter had found that the police had missed, perhaps there was more inside. But breaking and entering was a crime. And if he were caught, it would only make him look even more guilty. But something told Peter the answers were inside that house.

He headed towards the creaky back door with the broken screen basing against the frame in the small fall night's breeze. Peter almost fell into a firepit. A fresh one. It wasn't from Mr. Dalton. He had been killed the day before. The ashes in the grate must have been only a couple of hours old. Something still burned; had the killer tried to discard evidence? Why hadn't the police seen this sooner?

Pulling his penknife from his pocket, Peter poked through the ashes, and that's when he saw a charred envelope. Pulling out the latex gloves from his pocket, mindful not to get his fingerprints on what could be vital evidence, Peter extracted the message from inside the envelope.

'I know what you did. Pay....'

The rest of the message was already burned away. So, was this why Mr. Dalton was so hard up for cash? Was he being blackmailed? And what had Mr. Dalton done that was so bad to make him think he couldn't go to the police? How long had the poor man been suffering?

I wonder if there are any more of these notes inside? Peter thought.

Quickly snapping pictures of the boot prints and the note he found for evidence to protest his innocence, Peter prepared to go inside when, suddenly, the kitchen light flared to life. Ducking down into the flower bed, Peter watched for a shadow, a figure in the window. A clue as to who was inside and why.

Who was home? Had the true killer returned to destroy evidence? Peter didn't know, but he had nowhere else to go and didn't mind waiting to find out.

CHAPTER 9

alton Residence

Peter followed the light as it traveled through the house. With each light turned off, another would spring to life in another room. All the curtains were shut tight; no matter how close Peter got, he couldn't see who was inside. Whoever it was traveled upstairs and stayed there for a while. Peter checked his watch. It was almost five in the morning, and Peter had been observing the house nearly all night. He felt frozen to the bone.

Mindful to stay out of sight of the doorbell camera, Peter crept around the house. If he couldn't see anyone inside, he could at least watch whomever it was leave. Hiding in the bushes, Peter kept a close eye on the street; he didn't want any other neighbors to see him. But he needed a clear line of sight to Mr. Dalton's front door.

Finally, a tall, dark-haired man crept out the front door around five-thirty. Careful not to make a noise, the man closed the door behind him and locked it. Whomever it was had to be close to Mr. Dalton if he had a key. Was this the elusive missing son?

Peter tried to venture closer, but it was too risky. Any closer and he would be seen. The tall stranger turned his back to Peter and pulled his hood over his head, hiding his face before he left. A Black Porsche 911

GT3 touring sports car sat right out front. It was a pretty impressive piece of machinery; Peter couldn't understand how he had missed it. The car was at least one hundred thousand dollars easy. Was this the blackmailer?

Just as the stranger went to get in, Taylor emerged from her house in jogging gear, her eyes locked on the stranger across the street. The stranger swiftly returned a short nod of acknowledgment as he got in his car. The man drove off, and Taylor popped on her headphones and jogged off in the opposite direction.

Did these two know each other? Had Taylor purposefully given the police the footage to try and frame Peter to get the spot life off her? Was his original theory about Todd and Taylor having an affair right? Then, finally, things started to make sense. Taylor and her designer clothes, the mystery man in the luxury car, and the blackmail note. Deciding he couldn't wait another minute, Peter jogged to his car and headed to the police station.

CHAPTER 10

ine Grove Police Station

P As expected, the police station was quiet for that time of the morning. Charging right for the administration desk, Peter came across an officer who looked the least bit interested in being there.

"How can I help you?" asked the officer in the most unenthusiastic voice Peter had ever heard.

"I'm here to speak to the captain. Is he here?" Peter asked.

"He isn't in right now. Come back later," said the officer.

"Then call him and get him here. It is vital that I speak with him. It is regarding the Dalton case," Peter said a little more forcefully.

"Aren't you the guy accused of the murder?" asked the officer.

Looking closer, Peter could tell the officer was not long qualified. The young lad looked young enough to be fresh from the police academy.

"Can you just get the captain here?" Peter sighed, beginning to lose patience.

"Take a seat," huffed the officer picking up the phone to make a call.

Fifteen minutes later, the police captain walked into the station with large bags under his eyes, holding a cup of coffee from the gas station coffee machine on the edge of town.

"This better be important, Mr. Myers," the captain snipped, indicating Peter should follow him to the back.

"I wouldn't be here if it weren't," Peter answered.

The police captain led Peter to his office, closing the door and yawning loudly. His crinkled shirt was not fully tucked into his trousers, with the odd button done up in the wrong order.

"What is so important that I had to come in now?" the captain asked, sipping his bitter-smelling coffee as he sat opposite Peter at his desk.

"Do you have the autopsy report?" Peter asked.

"This is why you had me come down here? You have some nerve, Mr. Myers. You are interfering with a police investigation when you are already the prime suspect. I should book you for wasting police time," the captain snapped.

It was evident that the captain wasn't a morning person.

"I'm tired of your games, captain. You can't arrest me when you have nothing to go on. Do you have the autopsy report or not? I know my rights, and as a suspect, I have the right to know the details," Peter snapped.

"I have it somewhere," the captain frowned, searching through the chaos of papers and folders on his desk.

It was no wonder to Peter why the captain didn't seem to know what he was doing or get anything done when his desk was in such shambles. The man clearly didn't care about anything but himself. Peter couldn't understand how a man of the law could be so distant from his job.

"You haven't even looked at it, have you? I bet when you finally find that report, it will show the time of death was that night, proving my innocence. But, of course, it wouldn't surprise me if the footage from that time of night had been erased," Peter snapped.

Being a man who prides himself on putting bad guys behind bars, the captain's lack of enthusiasm and level of caring vexed Peter. It was rare that Peter was quick to anger, but something about the captain ticked all the boxes that angered Peter the most.

Scanning over several documents, the captain's face softened. He no longer looked angry to have been dragged to work in the early morning hours; he looked uneasy, almost embarrassed he had missed something so glaringly obvious.

"You are somewhat correct....the time of death was ten p.m.; our footage shows you leaving nine hours earlier......the footage from that time is...." the police captain stuttered.

"Gone?" Peter said, relaxing back in the chair and folding his arms across his chest.

Peter couldn't help looking as smug as he felt. He had known this police captain wasn't up to the job.

"Not gone; it appears the bad weather created power outages. Between the hours of nine-thirty and eleven-thirty, the doorbell camera glitched several times. Turning on and off again," the police captain reluctantly admitted.

"Or it was deliberately turned off," Peter suggested.

"Excuse me?" the captain asked, stunned he hadn't thought of it himself.

"I suggest you take a look at the Logans themselves, Taylor Logan in particular. And while you are at it, call in Todd Dalton, Mr. Dalton's son. I hear he is in town," Peter suggested rising to his feet.

"Todd Dalton is in town?"

"Yes, you may find it interesting that Greg Logan said perhaps Todd killed his father," Peter said.

Peter tossed his phone onto the table, preloaded with the pictures he had taken from the Dalton residence. The police captain's eyes widened in surprise.

"I don't want to tell you how to do your job, captain. But if I can find evidence in such obvious places, I don't know how you didn't. Footprints by the windows, a burning note in the backyard, and someone was at the house last night. Since you love doorbell cam footage so much, why not ask Taylor for the footage from half an hour ago? I'm sure it will shed some light on the situation," Peter said, grabbing his phone back and leaving without another word.

EPILOGUE

Gossip around town the following day was like fire spreading through a forest. No one could understand how Peter was cleared so easily and how the police captain had solved the crime. Apparently, Peter wasn't the only one to have noticed the captain's incompetence at times.

With the investigation no longer looming over his head and the answers to his questions finally answered, Peter could relax. No longer distracted by the prospect of going to prison for a crime he didn't commit, Peter invited Jessica out for a morning coffee.

They sat enjoying the gentle warmth of the October morning sun, both wrapped up in case of impending wind. Jessica had opted for a pumpkin spice latte; it was her favorite thing about fall, while Peter stuck to black coffee. Why mess with a classic?

"I'm in awe of the gossip surrounding us," Jessica smiled.

"Gossip?" Peter asked, intrigued.

"Yeah, the crazy vet willing to date a suspected murderer and the murder suspect who helped solve a crime."

"I haven't heard anyone suggest I helped solve it," Peter said.

"Well, they haven't, but I'm no fool. I know you had something to do with it. There is no way the police chief managed to solve it so quickly on his own. Let's say he has a reputation for taking credit for other people's work," Jessica winked.

Peter kept stumped, but his smug grin told Jessica all she needed to know.

"Go on then, tell me," Jessica said.

Peter explained how he and the police chief had discovered a foul plot afoot. The Logans and Todd Dalton had planned to kill Mr. Dalton together. When Greg had been laid off and Todd sacked for misconduct at the college in Oregon, the pair had met up when Todd came to town looking to get back into his father's good books.

"Back in his good books? What do you mean?" Jessica asked, enthralled with the details.

"Mr. Dalton and Todd had a falling out years ago, and Mr. Dalton had disowned his son, took him out of the Will, and stopped his inheritance," Peter answered.

"So, how were the Logans involved?"

Peter explained that Taylor and Todd went back years. And when she saw Todd with her husband, they concocted the blackmail plot.

"Ah, I see. So that explains why Taylor was suddenly sporting designer clothes and handbags," Jessica realized.

"And the new fancy doorbell that caught me leaving, she tried to use to pin the crime on me," Peter said.

"I'll admit, I never thought Taylor had it in her. She wasn't always the brightest bulb in the box," Jessica said, but not to be insulting. "So why kill him?"

"Once they rinsed the poor man dry, they were worried he would go the authorities about being watched. Everyone saw him with the shotgun. I mean, Mr. Dalton wasn't wrong. His son, a cruel man, was leaving blackmail notes where he would find them, kept the old man on edge for months," Peter tutted, feeling for Mr. Dalton.

"Did you find out what Dalton did? Wasn't he just a simple science teacher?" Jessica asked.

The answer was simple yet heartbreaking. Todd and the Logans had taken advantage of an old man's guilt and declining health.

"Todd's mother, Sylvia, had a lot of money; she was an heiress or something. Dalton inherited it all when she passed. Dalton blamed himself for not being there when she died, too busy working. He was never the same after that. Seeing his father's misplaced guilt and recognizing early onset Dementia, Todd saw how he could benefit since he was out of the Will."

"That's disgusting and heartbreaking. Poor Mr. Dalton," Jessica said, visibly upset by the tale.

Peter reached across the table, gently taking Jessica's hand. Instantly he felt a spark of electricity shoot through him, and from the look in her eyes, she had too.

"Let's change the subject to happier things," Peter smiled.

"I wish I could, but I better head off to work. Murder talk aside, this was fun," Jessica smiled gently, pressing her lips to Peter's cheek.

Jessica gave Sam a quick pat on the head and received a lick in thanks before she headed off to the vet clinic. Peter watched her leave. Like a schoolboy, he pressed his hand to his cheek. Jessica was something special.

"Woof! Woof! Woof!" Sam barked after her, a small sorrowful whimper at her departure, leaving his throat.

Peter wrapped his arms around Sam's neck, hugging the dog tightly.

"I know, boy, I'm sad to see her leave too, but who knows, maybe we will meet again soon," Peter hoped.

"Woof!" Sam barked in agreement.

Peter laughed softly at his four-legged friend, who brought so much joy into his life.

"Come on, boy. Let's go home," Peter smiled, leading the way.

Peter was in such a good mood that he decided to take the long way home. He wanted to enjoy the beauty of the crazy little town he called home. The mountains behind the town were framed by the stunning, ever-changing foliage of fall. The smell of the trees hung in the fall air. Even with a slight chill as winter approached, it was beautiful. Sam walked proudly at his side, Peter's new best friend. The few people around town who chose not to indulge in idle gossip waved and said hello. Peter waved back, wishing everyone a good day.

Life was beautiful; there was no way about it. But still, Peter had a sinking feeling that the blissful piece of Pine Grove would soon come to an end. What else did this tiny little town have in store for Peter and Sam? He had only been back at his family home for two months, the mayor was already cloaked in scandal, and Peter had been accused of murder.

Peter didn't dare ask the question of what else could go wrong; he did not want to scare or tempt fate. But one question he did want to ask was whether things would progress with Jessica. Her warm face, gentle eyes, and hearty laugh played in his memory. Dare Peter dream of a love connection? Either way, he was happy to have her in his life, whether as a love interest or just as a friend. He also knew that Sam loved her too, which meant he always had an excuse to see her.

Her gentle goodbye kiss still tickled his cheek, making Peter smile like a young boy again.

"She really is something, isn't she, boy?" Peter asked.

"Woof!" replied Sam, his tail wagging in agreement.

Without realizing it, Peter's mind wandered a little further to what his late mother would think of Jessica. His mother also loved animals. And knowing the type of person Jessica was, Peter was proud to say his mother would have loved her. It was such a shame that she had passed and never got a chance to meet her.

The End

Did you enjoy *Sweater Weather*?
Please consider rating it on Goodreads, Bookbub or your favorite retailer. Reviews help me reach new readers.

Read all the books in the Cozy Mystery Samplers.

Read all the stories
Jane and Kennedy Daniels Mysteries
Pine Grove Mysteries
Wilma Wade Holiday Mysteries
Mike and Maddie Mysteries

Mystic Moonhaven Mysteries
Annie Archer Paranormal Mysteries

Join my Newsletter for updates and giveaways!
www.daisylandishromance.com

www.ingramcontent.com/pod-product-compliance
Lightning Source LLC
Chambersburg PA
CBHW020340260626
47156CB00004B/1613